THE ICING ON THE CAKE

The Icing on the Cake

Sorcha Grace

Praise for A TASTE OF YOU

"With a deliciously sexy hero, a heroine with unforgettable spice, and mouthwatering sensuality, Sorcha Grace's *A Taste of You* will have you begging for seconds. Absolutely delectable."
— J. Kenner, *New York Times* bestselling author of RELEASE ME, CLAIM ME, and COMPLETE ME

"More than just a taste of sexy here. Scorching hot flames have burned up dinner! Witty and fun, *A Taste of You* by Sorcha Grace is a satisfying, sensual read not to be missed."
— Raine Miller, *New York Times* Bestselling Author

"Fans of Sylvia Day and E.L. James will find a lot to like about the mysterious William Lambourne and will root for a heroine who deserves a second chance at love. An intriguing start to a saucy new trilogy."
— Roni Loren, National bestselling author of FALL INTO YOU

"Yummy! Imagine Christian Grey with warm chocolate and you have William Lambourne. Add a complex heroine who gives love another try and you have *A Taste of You*. This steamy romance will take you through twists and turns and have you cheering for love to prevail. I can't wait to read what's next for William and Catherine!"
— Aleatha Romig, Author of the bestselling CONSEQUENCES series

THE ICING ON THE CAKE

Copyright © 2015 Sorcha Grace

To M, S, and D—You'll always be my deliciously ever after.

ONE

Thursday morning
Catherine

"Aw, hell," William groaned through his clenched jaw as his naked body writhed under me. His voice was raspy and not just from desire. He'd been sleeping rather soundly before I'd slid down and parked myself between his muscular thighs, intent on taking glorious advantage of his morning erection.

I continued to gently work William into my mouth, my tongue circling his thick shaft as he practically vibrated with arousal. I'd pulled back the bedcovers, so I could see the way his abs twitched and flexed when my lips passed over the engorged vein on his hard cock's underside. That spot always got him, so I teased and tantalized there a little bit more. I wanted him throbbing.

"*Fuuuuck*, Catherine." William's hands threaded through my hair as he pushed my head down toward his arching hips.

I sucked him in, taking him as deep as I could into my throat before pulling back, making sure I didn't miss a single inch of him. It was no easy feat, but I was intent on giving him The. Best. Blowjob. Ever. I was rarely up before him, especially these days, and I planned to show him why skipping the gym and sleeping in could be a good thing. Plus, I was madly, crazily, completely in love with the man I was pleasuring with my mouth, and I loved getting him off like this.

There was one more reason why I decided to go oral on *Mr.* Lambourne this morning: I was really hoping he'd return the favor.

William's hips began to pump, which meant he was close. I sucked harder, using my hand as well as my tongue to work his long, hard length. He groaned again, and I felt the answering beat in his cock.

"Oh yeah, oh fuck yeah," he practically growled as his grip on my messy ponytail tightened while his sweet release spilled into my mouth. I swallowed quickly, the taste of William making me smile. With one last pull that made him groan, I let go of him and licked my lips.

"Good morning," I purred and looked up at him through my lashes.

"Yes, it is, beautiful girl," he said in his gravelly morning voice. "Thanks for the wake up call." He gave me a sly smile.

A just-pleasured-and-naked William, with his tousled ebony hair and his stormy blue-grey eyes sizing me up hungrily, was sexy as hell, and I felt my nipples pull into tight, hard points in response. William's gaze dropped to my bare breasts. "What happened to your T-shirt? You were wearing one last night when we went to bed."

Before I could answer, he reached for me and pulled me close so we faced each other on the bed, my breasts pressed against his broad, bare chest. I was cocooned in his heat and my heart beat fast in anticipation. I ran my hands over his shoulders and the sculpted muscles of his back.

The terrace doors were open, and an early morning breeze scented with jasmine wafted through the room. Without the covers or my shirt, my bare skin pebbled with goosebumps, and William pulled me closer to him. Light filtered through the shutters, playing on the dark, rich colors of the walls and the ornately carved headboard above us. The bed was large enough to sleep four, but at the moment—my legs tangled with William's, his arms wrapped around me—it felt like the perfect size for the two of us.

He nuzzled my neck, making a trail of soft little kisses until he closed his mouth on mine, kissing me gently. His tongue darted out and along the top of my mouth, teasing, only to be replaced by his teeth nibbling at my lower lip. I sighed, and his tongue moved in to stroke mine, lazily at first and then with more heat. William was an excellent kisser, and normally I couldn't get enough. I usually loved to indulge in the mastery of his foreplay as much as anything, but this morning I wanted more. I *needed* more.

My breasts felt heavy, my nipples ached to be touched. As always, taking William's cock in my mouth had totally turned me on, and I knew I was already wet and ready. Every movement I made sent zings of awareness down through my belly and legs.

I wrapped my legs around his hips, pressing against him. William had more stamina than any human male had a right to, and I felt him harden again when I brushed against his cock. And then, just as I began to rub against him, he shifted slightly and broke contact. He was still kissing me, but he rose on one elbow and shifted his body, moving his hardness away from me. *Why was he doing this?*

Suddenly, the large bed felt much, much too big. I tried to nudge closer, but every time I did, William seemed to evade contact. *What the hell?* I pulled back. Obviously, I needed to be more direct. "Put your mouth on me, William," I murmured. "My nipples are so sensitive right now. I think I'll come if you touch them. Please. I want you so much." I was writhing and my voice was breathy and hot.

"I know," he said, before he made a sound low in his throat and…moved to kiss my neck again. To my annoyance, he didn't dip his lips any lower and his hands stayed on my arms and shoulders.

William loved my breasts. I couldn't believe he wasn't touching them, kissing them, or accepting my invitation to make me come by fondling them. I was so fucking turned on, I could hardly think straight, but every time I inched closer or tried to press more than my mouth against him, he moved back. It was almost comical except it wasn't funny.

At all.

Finally, I decided to make my desires crystal clear. "I want you so much. Your mouth, your cock. Please, make love to me." I pressed against him again.

William raised his head and looked down at me. A lock of his brown hair had fallen over his smooth forehead and his eyes were silvery grey under his dark brows. I knew this look and he was obviously as aroused as I was. His lips were slightly swollen from our kisses, and sun and shadow played over the chiseled planes of his cheeks. Whether taken in parts or as a whole, William Maddox Lambourne was an absolutely gorgeous male specimen, made all the more beautiful by the love that we shared.

"You don't know how tempting your invitation is," he said, his low voice rumbling through me and making me even hotter.

Until I realized he was about to turn me down.

"But we have a lot to do today."

He was saying no to sex.

And this wasn't the first time.

Before William could pull away, I wrapped my arms around his shoulders. "We do have a busy day. All the more reason to take advantage of the time we have now." I kissed him, then whispered, "And of me."

He kissed me back briefly and looked down at me again, his eyes now that icy cold negotiator blue that meant his mind was made up. "It's getting late." He disentangled himself and rolled to the side of the bed and sat up. "The wedding guests are going to be arriving for the weekend today, and I need to make sure we're ready."

It was a good thing his back was to me else he would have seen my giant eye roll. I bit my tongue before I could point out that Casa di Rosabela, William's grand estate home nestled on a hillside in his Napa Valley vineyard, had an entire staff devoted to ensuring the house was ready for the wedding.

"I'm going to grab a quick shower and see how things are coming along." Then he stood up and walked, totally naked, toward the white marble bathroom with its sunken tub and luxurious shower, but not before he picked my T-shirt up off the floor and tossed it over to me.

I slipped it back on, then flopped back on the pillows, closed my eyes, and groaned. What was it called when a woman had the equivalent of blue balls? Seriously, I was so hot and bothered I was on the verge of some kind of a breakdown. All those kisses on my neck, William's tongue stroking mine, my mouth on his big hard cock. I was completely worked up and he knew it—hell, I couldn't have offered myself to him more obviously—yet he'd walked away. What kind of sadist was he?

Sometimes a girl had to take things into her own hands. I let my hand wander down my stomach and into my panties, which were damp with my arousal. My fingers glided through my slick folds and I felt the heat radiating from my core. I put two fingers on my clit, which was so engorged it almost hurt, and pressed. It wouldn't take much to find my own release, but I couldn't stop my thoughts from returning to William.

Why did he keep pushing me away?

TWO

I gave up on getting myself off and pulled the soft covers around me, propping myself up on the pillows. I felt sort of silly in the giant bed all alone. I didn't even have Laird to keep me company. Yesterday, he'd been dispatched to Puppy Acres, a swanky pet "resort" that promised to give my pooch the dog vacation of a lifetime while the wedding festivities got underway here. I'd bet he wasn't missing me at all.

I did love this bedroom. It was really a bedroom *suite*, since the sitting room and the closet adjoined the spacious main room. The bathroom was huge and about half the size of my entire condo in Lincoln Park, so it counted as a room by itself, too.

Even though Casa di Rosabela was oversized and luxurious, I didn't feel half as awkward here as I did in William's Chicago penthouse. Maybe it was because I grew up in California, and St. Helena felt more like home to me than Chicago. Maybe it was because I loved the Old World charm of the 1920s house or that the décor was so warm and colorful—the complete antithesis of William's museum-like place in the Windy City that bordered on sterile. Whatever it was, I didn't want to be anywhere else.

And if anyone had told me four weeks ago that I'd be here,

14

preparing for a wedding, I wouldn't have believed it. Mostly because the past month had felt more like a year and my life had changed so much. But it really had only been four weeks since William showed up at my hotel in Paris.

Four weeks since I found out I was pregnant.

And four weeks since we'd last had sex.

I let out another frustrated sigh. The sun, now streaming through the terrace doors, glinted off the giant engagement ring on my left hand. It was enormous, and the most beautiful thing I'd ever seen. At nearly seven carats, the emerald-cut diamond had a slight pink tint that reminded me of a piece of bubblegum.

Really expensive bubblegum.

I tilted the ring so the light caught the flawless stone and then glimmered off the exquisite platinum setting edged in equally flawless tiny diamonds. I loved my ring, and I loved William. I still felt giddy when I remembered that night at the Hotel Plaza Athénée. I'd been so shocked to see him and then startled when he asked if I would take him back. I'd really thought we were through, but William had apologized and told me he'd love me forever. That he had loved me from the moment he saw me.

I was The One for him.

Of course I took him back. I'd never wanted anything as much in my entire life.

And then he had found *Le EPT* in a white paper bag sitting on a table. I'd finally bought a pregnancy test, mainly to shut Beckett up but also because there were too many signs for even me to ignore.

William had been surprised, that's for sure, but he'd insisted I take the test right then. I'd been so glad to have him by my side, but terrified, too.

There had been no going back, no more sticking my head in the sand. I'd gone into the opulent bathroom and peed on the stick. William had held my hand and stared into my eyes while we waited to see if a blue plus sign would appear. Neither of us spoke, and when I finally lifted the test, with shaking hands, the plus sign had sent a wave of dread through me. I'd then dropped the stick and fought to keep my dinner down.

The bathroom had seemed to spin until I caught a glimpse of William's face in the mirror. He'd caught the stick and was smiling, his expression one of pure joy. Laughing, he'd pulled me into his arms and he'd held me until I felt steady again.

"You're okay with this?" I'd asked when the room had stopped tilting. I'd held my breath, waiting for his answer.

"I'm more than okay, Catherine. I love you and we're having a baby. I'm going to be a father. It's incredible." His voice had broken on the last word and I saw the sheen of tears in his beautiful blue eyes.

I had been so scared, but William had never stopped stop smiling. He told me over and over how wonderful it all was as I'd continued to tremble in his arms. And then he'd started to kiss me, to worship me, really. Soft kisses that had started on my nape and that became more intense as he made his was down to my sensitive breasts, then to my belly and on down to my inner thighs, and then right to my very center. He'd carried me back to the bed and went on to show me just how wonderful he thought I was, and just how much he loved me. It was like our hearts and minds had joined with our bodies. I'd never felt as connected to someone as I did to William that night, as we took each other back and celebrated what we'd created.

And that was the last time we'd had sex. Four weeks ago. William hadn't been inside me since that night in Paris, despite all of my efforts to persuade him.

Frustration washed over me again, and I dropped my hand with the ring on the bed and flopped back against the pillows.

*****

William emerged from the master closet freshly showered and dressed. I could smell his signature scent across the room, and I bit my lip to dial back my arousal. If I couldn't convince him to take me when we were naked in bed together; he definitely wasn't going to take off the clothes he'd just put on so he could ravish me. He wore a tight T-shirt topped with a denim button-down. He'd rolled up the sleeves and left the shirt open over his broken-in cargo shorts. In place of his usual Italian black wingtips he wore scuffed work boots. A pair of aviator sunglasses was perched on top of his head.

The man looked like sex personified.

I absolutely loved casual William, and I was finally getting used to him starting his work days dressed like this rather than in one of his London bespoke suits. It was hard to believe, but William the vintner might have even been sexier than William Maddox

Lambourne, the billionaire business mogul. I'd never realized how sexy happiness could be, but it truly was the best accessory. William was so much more carefree now, and his passion for his work was evident in the way he carried himself and in the lack of tension in his shoulders.

I still couldn't believe how lucky I was to be engaged to the man standing in front of me. Sure, he was rich and gorgeous, but more than that, he seemed content and at peace. He was exactly the man I wanted to spend the rest of my life with. I just needed to figure out why he was avoiding having sex with me.

William crossed to the bed and sat. I could smell his soap more strongly now, and I had to resist the urge to crawl to him and start licking. His hair had grown since Paris and I loved the way it curled along the nape of his neck. All the time spent outside in the California sun had given him a bit of a tan, too. I blew out a breath and struggled to take another in. He was so hot that sometimes I had to remind myself to breathe.

"I'll be out in the vineyard this morning," he said, oblivious to my struggles to refrain from slobbering all over him. "I have to supervise some repairs to the irrigation system, then I'll come in and direct the event planners on the set-up."

I barely heard a word he said since I was too occupied enjoying the sexy way his mouth moved.

"I'll send Fernanda up with some breakfast and juice. You need to eat. Catherine?"

"I know," I said after a beat, my mind finally tuning into the conversation.

He took my hand and rubbed a thumb over my knuckles. "Come out and join me if you feel like it. Or not. Take it easy today, baby." He leaned over and kissed me again, a soft sweet kiss that left me wanting much, much more. "I love you, but I've got to get going."

I reached to wrap my arms around him and pull him close, but he was already up and halfway out of the room. With a moan, I covered my eyes. This was torture.

I started to drift off again as I thought back to Paris and fashion designer Fiona Joy's fashion show. The post-show dinner was the whole reason I'd been in Paris. William, being William, had miraculously wrangled an invitation to the event. He'd wanted to be close to me and yet he'd given me a respectful distance while I photographed the whole night. I felt energized knowing he was there, but also so very overwhelmed by everything that has happened earlier that day: William back in my life and a baby on the way. All of it was too much.

World-class chef Hutch Morrison and my pseudo "boss"— who would be arriving at Casa di Rosabela later this morning—had been brilliant, as always, and the dinner had been spectacular. Even William had been impressed by Hutch's culinary prowess, and that was no easy feat. I'd been so distracted that I had worried how my photos of the food and of Hutch in action would turn out, but they, too, were amazing. I had a whole slew of new job offers sitting in my inbox thanks to Hutch and Fiona's show, but I hadn't agreed to any new assignments yet. I felt too…unsettled. How could I say yes to a job with so many things up in the air?

And now we'd been in California for two weeks, and William hadn't shown any sign of wanting to go back to Chicago. For the most part, these past two weeks had felt like an extended vacation, but we had to get back to our real lives at some point, right? I didn't know if Chicago was still home or if we were based in California now. And, *hello*? I was literally a ticking clock.

Getting pregnant had not been in my plan and it had definitely not been part of any of the future-with-William scenarios I'd allowed myself to fantasize about. The news wasn't officially out yet, but I could already imagine all the gossip that would go down once it was. Getting knocked up by Chicago's most eligible bachelor after dating him for less than three months looked opportunistic, even to me. Plus, the press was going to have a field day with the news since Elin Erickson's arrest had become a national news story. Headlines like *PSYCHO SPINSTER TARGETS BILLIONAIRE'S LATEST BABE* weren't going away. I knew William's "people" were on it and doing their best to deflect attention away from us, but once it got out that I was William's *pregnant* babe, the tabloids were going to go crazy.

I just didn't want William's family to think this was some stunt I'd pulled to trap him. They mattered so much to him, which meant their opinion of *me* mattered a lot to him, too. Zoe Smith, William's favorite cousin, pretty much hated my guts, so I was already counting on her to be as negative as possible. Maybe keeping our distance from Chicago and keeping a low profile was intentional on William's part?

A quick knock sounded on the door, and I pulled the covers up and tried to look awake. "Come in!"

"Good morning, Miss Catherine." William's housekeeper, Fernanda, entered with a bright smile and a tray with a carafe of orange juice and a colorful plateful of food. "How are you feeling today?"

"Great," I managed, but just one whiff of the spinach and feta omelet made my stomach churn violently. I tried not to breathe so Fernanda wouldn't catch on. It was a picture perfect healthy breakfast—a fluffy omelet garnished with fresh fruit and sprigs of parsley. Even the champagne flute with my juice had an orange wedge on the rim.

I smiled through the nausea and tried to swallow the bile that rose in my throat. "Thanks, Fernanda," I said when she placed the tray on the bed. "This looks delicious."

And it totally did. But unfortunately, the gourmet cuisine at William's villa was no match for my morning sickness. Thankfully, Fernanda included a side of dry wheat toast, so at least I could I nibble on that.

She gave me a knowing look before bustling back out the door. I didn't feel like eating, but I also knew I'd need all my strength to get through today. I picked up the toast and took a deep breath. "Here we go."

THREE

The toast went a long way in settling my stomach, and, suddenly hungry, I ate most of the spinach and feta omelet. That seemed to be the way with my pregnancy. One moment I couldn't imagine eating anything, the next I was ravenous.

After breakfast, I pulled on a knee-length, pale yellow skirt that swished when I walked, a soft grey T-shirt, and a cute pair of ballet flats. I'd spent most of the Chicago winter dressed in layers upon layers of black and grey, so some color was a nice change for spring in California. Plus my jeans were getting a little too tight, so I was wearing a lot of loose, flowy, feminine clothes that didn't hug my body too much. I swear that I'd also already gone up nearly a full cup size, so I needed to do some bra shopping soon. I couldn't see a baby bump yet, thank goodness, though I checked every time I passed a mirror.

The day had dawned sunny and warm with a light breeze, and I took my time strolling through the halls of Casa di Rosabela. William's home looked lovely at night, but it was even more spectacular during the day. This morning I lingered to admire one of my favorite things here: a Monet that hung over the fireplace in the living room. It was a small but exquisite rendering of a pond of water lilies beneath an arched wooden bridge. And it was

22

breathtaking—as was that fact that I was standing in William's living room, not in a museum, looking at a real Monet that was surely worth millions. No matter how much I loved William, I'd never get used to his staggering wealth.

I knew everyone would be in the kitchen—and by everyone I meant Beckett—so I left the art behind and made my way to that wing of the villa. Beckett had insisted on making the cake himself, so I knew he'd be up measuring and mixing. He was an extraordinary pastry chef and a total control freak when it came to his craft and I so loved that about him. I knew Alec did, too.

It was still hard for me to believe that Beckett and Alec were getting married—and in just two days' time. When I'd come back from Paris, ready to tell Beckett all of my news, he had stolen my thunder big time. Turned out that once *he'd* gotten back to Chicago from Paris, he'd wasted no time in declaring his love for Alec, who told him that he'd never had any doubt that Beckett was the guy for him. Then Beckett had told me they were getting married.

Just like that.

Beckett said he just *knew*, and Alec had always known. Who could argue? Not me. I was deliriously happy for both of them and thrilled that William had agreed to host their wedding at Casa di Rosabela.

Every time I thought about *my* engagement, I couldn't help but look down at my ring. It should have felt heavy on my finger due to its size, but really it carried a burden for a whole other reason. Beckett didn't have an engagement ring, but he had something I lacked: an eagerness to walk down the aisle.

For Beckett, it was simple. He was totally in love with Alec and he couldn't wait to marry him. Seeing the two of them so excited about joining their lives together was almost infectious.

Almost.

For me, it was complicated. Yes, I was totally in love with William and I loved the *idea* of marrying him, but I was definitely in no hurry. In fact, I was more or less dragging my feet about setting a date. I told myself I just wanted to enjoy being engaged for a while, but the truth was, since Paris, things had been different between us—and this morning was just more proof of that. Maybe it was because I was pregnant or maybe it was because of something else. I didn't really know since William seemed to be avoiding talking to me about anything important.

William was not a "go with the flow" kind of a man. He was just the opposite, in fact. He always got exactly what he wanted and he had the determination, intelligence, and means to accomplish just about anything. Which meant this was how he wanted things for now. He seemed at peace, but I was anything but.

The uncertainty was making me crazy. We needed to decide on a home. We needed to talk about my work. We needed to talk about the baby and about why we weren't having sex. We needed to talk about all of it and about our hopes and our fears, too. Or maybe it was just my fears, since William didn't seem worried at all. That scared me, too.

And if I were being honest with myself, I knew that part of

the reason I was freaking out had to do with Jace.

I paused in front of one of the large windows overlooking the vineyards and sighed. No matter how far I had come since Jace's death in that terrible accident five years earlier, no matter the love and happiness I had been so damned lucky to find again, the pain of that terrible loss never left me. Nor did the fear that everything would all be snatched away from me again.

I stared out at the green fields bathed in golden sunlight, which reminded me of the morning in Paris when William proposed, the morning after the Fiona Joy dinner. I'd wanted to order room service, but William had argued that we couldn't eat room service in Paris, not when there was so much great food at our fingertips. We had to get out and enjoy the city. I'd reluctantly agreed and then William took me to a beautiful outdoor café. A section of the café had been fashioned into a flowering garden that overlooked the Seine, and William had led me by the hand into the fragrant retreat. I still don't know how William had managed it, but a special table had been reserved just for us, set with delicate flowered china and gleaming silver.

William had ordered *café au lait* and warm *pain au chocolat* and it had been perfect. And then, over the fragrant blend of flowers, coffee, and chocolate, he'd lowered himself to one knee.

I'd gasped, knowing what he was about to do but shocked nonetheless. It had all seemed so surreal, surrounded as we had been by the lilting French in the voices of people strolling along the Seine and the distant bells of Notre Dame.

"Catherine." He'd taken my hand and looked into my eyes. I couldn't ever resist him when he looked at me that way, with those perfectly blue eyes that seemed to see right into my heart and soul. "I love you."

"I know—" I'd begun, but he hadn't let me interrupt.

"Before I met you, my world was all noise that echoed in an emptiness I didn't even know was there. You came into my life, and the noise turned into music. The black and white of my world transformed to color. You filled the emptiness with your laughter, your smile, and your love. I didn't know what love was before I met you. You've taught me to love, and I've fallen more deeply in love with you than I thought possible."

Tears had stung my eyes as every word he spoke warmed my heart. I'd started to tell William I felt the same, but he'd spoken again.

"I swear to you now—no, I *vow* to you that I will love you with my whole heart until the end of my life and beyond. Catherine." He squeezed my hand. "I told you before I wanted to marry you when you were ready. I want that now more than ever. You're having my baby, *our* baby. I want you to be my wife and I want to start our family the right way. Catherine, will you marry me?"

I'd squeezed his hand back, overwhelmed with emotion. And as much as I knew he loved me, I hadn't been able to shake the feeling that he was proposing only because I was pregnant. I'd been about to tell William all of this and then I'd looked into his eyes. They were clear and blue and shone when he looked at me. His smile had been so warm and his expression so earnest. At that moment, my heart had felt so full of love that I could hardly speak.

Beckett always said I was the world's worst over-thinker and I'd decided right then that I wasn't going to let my overthinking ruin what was probably the most romantic moment of my life. Without further hesitation, I'd thrown myself into his arms.

"Yes!" I'd cried. "Yes, I'll marry you." I'd kissed him furiously, tears streaming down my cheeks until I could taste their saltiness on our joined lips.

Later that morning, William had whisked me off to Cartier, which was like a glittering wonderland. Tray after tray of diamond rings and loose diamonds had been placed before me.

"Choose whatever you like, beautiful girl," William had murmured in my ear, his hand warm and firm around mine.

I'd stared at the assortment of jewels, stunned and overwhelmed. Jace had never given me an engagement ring. We'd both worn simple and very plain wedding bands. But an engagement ring was important to William, though all I cared about was the man himself.

"You pick," I'd said, looking up at him. The words had felt right. "You choose for me."

And he had.

I held the ring up to the window and admired it yet again. It was a vintage piece, which I loved, and the stone had a history and a title. The jeweler at Cartier had told us it was called the Frangipani Diamond.

I loved the name, so warm and exotic, like the jewel itself. When William had slipped the ring on my finger, he'd whispered that the color reminded him of his favorite parts of me. I'd blushed furiously, and I could feel my cheeks heating even now as I remembered how his throaty whisper had made me wet.

I still had no idea how much the ring had cost. I tilted my hand again, staring at the beautiful piece of jewelry that was likely worth a few *decades* of my annual salary. It glittered and caught the light as it resided on my ring finger like a sparkling pink weight.

I don't know how long I stood there before I realized I'd wasted too much time daydreaming—an all-too common thing since becoming pregnant—and finally made my way to the kitchen.

FOUR

As I'd suspected, Beckett was in William's favorite room, starting the process of making his own wedding cake.

"There she is. Sleeping Beauty." He gave me a quick hug before going back to the task of measuring dry ingredients. I leaned on the counter and watched him for a few moments, amazed at how calm he seemed given the magnitude of the weekend ahead of him.

"You could have hired that out, you know," I told him, loving how this little jab would get him going.

"Don't remind me," he said, being overly dramatic. "But you know I'd be here supervising anyway, so…might as well put the funds to good use. Like a dream honeymoon."

"Can I help with anything?" I asked.

Beckett gave me a look. "Just stay right where you are, and don't touch my cake." His tone was light, but he wasn't joking around. Beckett wanted this cake to be perfect, which was why he wouldn't allow anyone else to make it.

"Fine. I'll just sit here and watch."

"Smart move. Wouldn't want any flour to tarnish that glow you have going."

I touched my cheek. After my earlier bout of nausea, I didn't feel glowing.

"You and that fiancé of yours are certified sex maniacs—not that the results of what appear to have been multiple orgasms don't suit you."

"Ha! I wish."

Beckett lifted the baking powder and his brow.

"We're not sex maniacs lately," I muttered. "William has really been keeping his distance."

And his hands-off approach was starting to make me paranoid. I missed our intimacy. Our white-hot chemistry had kept us anchored through all the crazy shit we'd been through. First there was the misunderstanding about his dossiers on eligible women he might date, then about Jeremy, then Elin Erickson and the extortion scheme, not to mention William having to face the fact that he never going to know what had caused the plane crash that had killed his parents and brother all those years ago. We'd been through hell during the short time that we'd been together and our physical connection had kept us grounded.

Until this past month.

I could admit that William had been wise to keep his distance on a few bad days. I'd been weepy, exhausted, and nauseous on and off for weeks leading up to the trip to Paris. I'd tried to deny my suspicions, blaming my symptoms on the threats that required me to move into William's penthouse for protection. Then William and I had broken up and I'd been devastated. Who doesn't feel like complete shit after having her heart ripped out of her chest and stomped on? I'd expected to feel bad and I had.

But after I'd seen Elin Erickson behind bars, awaiting trial, and then William and I had reunited, I didn't have stress as an excuse for how sick I'd felt. Paris had been like a picture book fairy tale until the pregnancy test confirmed what I'd believed was impossible. After that, it was like the dam broke. Morning sickness had attacked with a vengeance—afternoon and evening sickness, too. I'd spent our last day in Paris in the hotel room, in bed, newly engaged but feeling swollen and achy everywhere. I'd been too exhausted to do more than roll over and whenever I did move, I'd felt sick to my stomach.

William—sweet, sweet William—had stayed by my side, making sure I sipped ginger ale and coaxing me to eat a few pieces of dry toast. He'd tried to cheer me up, even when my tears must have seemed incomprehensible. A few times, when he didn't think I was looking, I caught expressions of worry and concern on his face.

The next day I'd felt well enough to travel, and we'd said a hasty goodbye to Beckett and flew back to Chicago on William's private jet. I was the one not interested in sex then and visiting the mile high club had been the last thing on my mind. I'd slept the sleep of the dead the entire flight.

My doctor's appointment a few days later had been the final end to the fantasy. Apparently, my symptoms were completely normal for being almost eight weeks pregnant. I'd counted back after that revelation and figured I'd gotten pregnant right around Valentine's Day. But neither William nor I could relax because the fact was that I'd gotten pregnant with my IUD still in place.

The doctor had performed an ultrasound and confirmed the IUD was still inside me. She then explained that it had to come out. Immediately. The procedure would raise the chance of miscarriage but leaving it in was an even greater risk to me and the baby.

William and I had exchanged terrified looks, but he'd clasped my hand and held it firmly as I nodded and gave my consent.

Thankfully the removal itself had been quick and relatively painless. I'd gone home that afternoon with orders to rest and take it easy. *No sex for a week.*

My follow-up visit a week later put my immediate fears to rest. The baby was fine. I was fine. I could resume all of my normal activities, which I had.

Except one. Sex. And I was okay now. We were *both* okay now. Better than okay, in fact, but William was still treating me like I was on lock-down.

We'd agreed to keep the news to ourselves for the first trimester. I'd told Beckett, of course, but he was the only other person who knew. I hadn't even told my mother. The side effect of keeping my pregnancy a secret was that it almost didn't feel real. I never forgot I was pregnant—the moments of nausea, my more than bountiful cleavage, and the tiny hard curve I felt on my lower belly were reminders—but William and I didn't talk about it. Whenever I brought up the baby, he skirted the subject.

I hadn't anticipated his behavior, though I could hardly blame him when for a while everything had been so scary and fragile. His face had looked absolutely devastated when the doctor told us about the chance for a miscarriage. He'd held my hand tightly, but I'd felt the way his fingers trembled. But even now, weeks after the doctor had said all was well, it was as though he didn't believe it. He encouraged me to rest and eat, but that was it. It seemed like he was worried that if he allowed himself to be excited about our baby, it would hurt all the more if we lost him or her after all.

I understood all of that and I'd felt it too. But I also felt like I'd been pretending I wasn't pregnant for too long. I still really *was* pregnant, and it was time I embraced it. Morning sickness aside, I felt pretty good. I felt sexy and luscious and like everything about me was just a little bit *more*. I wanted to share it all with William, but how many times did I need to tell him I was okay before he actually believed it?

On top of everything else, there was our engagement. We hadn't kept *that* a secret. Our families and all of our friends had been so excited, and William's Aunt Abigail and my parents had all immediately started asking me about the wedding plans.

I'd ducked and dodged like a prizefighter. How could I start planning a wedding when all my thoughts were occupied with the baby William and I would be having before the end of the year, the baby that nobody knew about? I wasn't so sure everybody would be so excited once they found out the bride would be wearing a maternity wedding dress.

It wasn't just Abigail and my mom asking me about a wedding date. William had started nudging me, too. I could avoid discussions as expertly as he could, though. I'd managed to get around the conversation, but I had a feeling Beckett's wedding this weekend would make putting off the discussion much longer all but impossible.

"If he's keeping his distance, maybe he's concerned about how well you're feeling," Beckett said, sounding very far away. "Cat, hello?" Beckett chirped, snapping his fingers and bringing me back to the moment. "So tell me, how are you *feeling*?" He winked at me.

Of course Beckett wasn't afraid to chat about my pregnancy when we were alone. It was only William who was acting like it wasn't a reality. I was so tired of the whole fucked up situation. All of the websites I haunted when I was by myself said that this was supposed to be a happy time, not a neurotic one that inspired uncomfortable silences and worried glances.

"Just fine," I told Beckett. "I *feel* fine."

I could see the signs. I was about to get testy with Beckett, and I so couldn't allow that to happen during his wedding weekend. I shook it off and smiled. "How about we go over the guest list one more time?"

Unlike me, Beckett couldn't wait to talk about his wedding. I found the list on a counter out of the way and started ticking off names. Finally, I paused. "Are your parents coming?"

Beckett measured the salt intently, his eyes not meeting mine. "I'm not sure," he said, pouring it into the large mixing bowl. "My sister is coming, but my parents are still a *we shall see*."

I started to say something sympathetic to Beckett, but he interrupted. "So who else is on there? We already covered everyone from the bakery, right?"

We went down the list, Beckett mixing and measuring without missing a beat. When we finished, he excitedly launched into a lecture about the ingredients. The vanilla extract was from Madagascar, and he'd brought some of kind special sugar imported from Germany because it had the best structural integrity for cakes. As always, my eyes started to glaze over when Beckett discussed topics like the structural integrity of sugar—I knew he was into this stuff, but seriously? I glanced out the kitchen window and couldn't stop the grin that spread over my face at what I saw.

William was talking to Hutch Morrison near the vineyard.

FIVE

Hutch looked every inch the bad boy chef he was with his distressed leather duffel slung over his shoulder and a black leather roll in his hands, which I knew from past experience contained his knives. A world-class chef like Hutch didn't go anywhere without his personal tools of the trade. I forgot all about Madagascar vanilla and organic sugar and admired the two hot, handsome men talking animatedly in the morning sun.

William had his hands on his hips and his aviators were shading his eyes. He looked completely at ease on his land and so completely hot. Hutch was hot too, but it was William who drew my gaze over and over. I was his and had been from the first moment we met on that cold January night, when I'd tripped and spilled my camera gear all over the sidewalk in front of Willowgrass. Watching him, my anxiety started to melt away. My heart was completely and utterly owned by him, and I let that thought settle over me. I knew that William would never intentionally hurt me and he would do just about anything to make me happy. I vowed then and there to tell him I needed him, that we needed to talk, so I could put all my fears to bed. We'd just have to get through Beckett's special weekend first.

Outside the window, the two men shook hands and then William moved back toward the fields and Hutch started for the house. I watched William walk, admiring his ass, before turning my attention to the door as Hutch sauntered in.

"Hutch!" I said and jumped up to give him a hug.

"Lambourne said I'd find you inside, Miss Kitty Cat. How are you?" He kissed me on the cheek and then shook hands with Beckett. "Good to see you, too, man. I guess they already put you to work."

"It's a labor of love," Beckett said, capping his vanilla, lest any be spilled.

"Can I get you anything?" I offered.

"I would kill for coffee, darlin'."

"Um..." I glanced around, clueless. I'd switched to drinking herbal tea. "I know there must be coffee somewhere."

Beckett rolled his eyes. "I'll get it for you."

Hutch leaned one hip on the counter. "It's a good thing you're so gorgeous, Miss Kitty Cat, because a man can't count on you to feed him."

"Hey, no man of mine has ever gone hungry."

Hutch took a steaming cup from Beckett and gave me a simmering look over the rim. "I bet not. You're as delicious as ever."

"Oh, please." I waved my huge ring. "You'd choke on this if you got too close."

Hutch sipped his coffee. "Just because you're taken doesn't mean I can't look." He glanced around the kitchen and gave a low whistle. "This is some set-up. I should have known Lambourne's kitchen would be top of the line. I don't have a La Cornue Grand

Palais at my place," he said, referring to the large 6-burner range that ran along one wall of the kitchen. I'd never given it a second thought.

"That's a $50,000 oven right there. Doesn't get much better than that."

"I could live here," Beckett sighed. "In fact, I might just move in. It's big enough that no one would notice for months. "

Hutch chuckled. "You'll have to postpone those moving plans until after I work my culinary magic. This kitchen is mine until your wedding is over. I just needed a shot of coffee to fortify me. I'm planning something special for you and Alec." He set his coffee cup down. "I hope you don't mind, but I've called in reinforcements for the weekend."

Hutch was trying to sound serious and grave, but the smile on his lips revealed the fact that he was excited to share his big secret.

I decided to play along. "Ooh…who is it?" I asked.

"Kellan Thomas." Hutch announced, pausing for effect. "Ever heard of him?"

Neither Beckett nor I dared to move or breathe. Even *I* knew who Kellan Thomas was, and I knew hardly anything about the food world. He was only the most lauded chef in the United States and one of the very top chefs in the entire world. His signature restaurant, Oro, was in nearby Calistoga and it was legendary, but he had several others, too. He'd also published a ton of cookbooks and I knew who he was because his cookbook, *Oro a Casa,* was one of the only ones my mother owned. She used it every Thanksgiving.

Hutch's mouth curved in a grin that said he knew he'd just

stunned us and he'd thoroughly enjoyed the surprise. "I'm supposed to meet him in town in about an hour and then we're heading off to some farmers' markets. Anyone want to come along?" he drawled.

"I do!"

We all turned at the new voice as Zoe, William's cousin and the same one who despised me, strolled in the kitchen. "Great," I muttered under my breath.

Zoe and Beckett were cordial enough but they were hardly friends. Even so, Beckett had invited her to the wedding once he'd learned she had already been planning to stay at Casa di Rosabela this weekend before heading down to Oakland for a regatta. She was the coxswain for an internationally ranked Men's 8 rowing team, which was probably the most bizarre job I'd ever heard of.

Zoe looked simultaneously cute and sexy in cut-off shorts and a tank top, but I stifled a little gasp when I saw her. She was petite and her lithe, tightly muscled body was that of an athlete, but it was the sleeve of tattoos that covered her left arm that surprised me. I'd only met her twice and though I hadn't missed the small diamonds studs in her nose and eyebrow, I'd never seen her arms bared. William had never told me she was so heavily inked. And her tattoos were *beautiful*. I stared at the beautifully detailed tale of a golden-haired mermaid that wrapped around her bicep and seemed to ripple as she moved her arm.

To her credit, Zoe seemed completely oblivious to my reaction. Inked or not, she was effortlessly gorgeous with barely any makeup and her blond hair pulled back in a messy but artful ponytail.

I vowed again to be friendly.

"Hey, Zoe. Welcome." I pasted on a big smile.

"I'd love to go to the market with you, Hutch," she answered, not looking at me once as she said it. She couldn't keep her eyes off of Hutch.

"And I would love the company," Hutch said with a wink. "Come on, Miss Zoe. Let's go get us some vegetables." He gestured to the door and they headed out. I heard Zoe tell him they could choose a car from William's collection.

"Do you think their tattoos match?" Beckett asked, looking a little awestruck. "And was it just me or did she just totally blow you off?"

I rolled my eyes "It wasn't just you."

I had no idea what had happened between Zoe and Hutch since Beckett's St. Patrick's Day party at The Webster—practically a lifetime ago to me—but something was definitely brewing between those two. Hutch was a great guy and sexy as hell, but he'd been nursing a broken heart for a seriously long time. Zoe hardly seemed like a person who could be trusted to be gentle with him. She'd crush him, I was sure.

Beckett squealed and grabbed my shoulders. "Can you even believe it?"

"Zoe and Hutch?"

"Who cares about them?" He waved a hand. "Kellan Thomas! I have to keep pinching myself. I never thought I'd be lucky enough to find anyone who loved me enough to marry me, and

I sure as hell never dreamed my wedding would be catered by Hutch Morrison and Kellan fucking Thomas." He hugged me. "It's all because of you, Cat."

I hugged him back. "All because of me?"

"If you hadn't tripped on that sidewalk and met ol' *Stormy Eyes*, we'd still be cabbing it through the snow and eating at Kuma's."

I gave him a playful punch. "Hey, there's nothing wrong with Kuma's." Suddenly I found myself craving a burger in the most primal way.

Beckett rolled his eyes.

"Fine. I'll be serious. Beckett, I couldn't be more thrilled for you." I hugged him, and he gave me a bone-crunching hug back.

Six

My mother knew how to throw a party. Though I didn't have many memories of her, the ones I did possess were crystal clear. One night, when I'd had a bad dream or something, I'd gone downstairs and found her seated at the large kitchen island on a stool. She was wrapped in a robe, and had a glass of wine on the counter and a pile of cookbooks open in front of her. She'd asked me what I was doing up and we'd started talking. When I'd asked why she wasn't in bed, she said she couldn't sleep. She'd been tossing and turning all night, trying to figure out the perfect side dish for the beef tenderloin she would be serving at a dinner party later in the week. Then, *voila*, inspiration had struck and beckoned her to the kitchen, to the recipe, but she couldn't remember which cookbook it was in. She'd laughed, warm and vibrant with her blue-grey eyes—*my* eyes—crinkling up at the edges. I'd laughed, too and said that it was only meat, what did it matter? "Oh, William," she'd said as she ruffled my hair. "One day you'll learn it's all about making an impression."

I'd say I got my desire to leave people in awe from her. These days the only person I cared about impressing was my future wife. There was nothing I loved more than putting a smile on

Catherine's face, which was why I was going all out this weekend for Beckett and Alec. Beckett was a friend and I admired him as a professional, but I was doing this because he meant the world to Catherine. If Catherine was happy, I was happy. I'd seen entirely too much sorrow and terror in her eyes since we'd met. All of the shit that went along with being with me—my fucked-up childhood, my money, the round-the-clock security I required, Elin Erickson and her insane attempts to harm me and the people I loved—she'd been hurt by all of it. I regretted it every day, which was why keeping her in California, calm and happy, healthy and safe, was all that I cared about anymore.

A vision flashed into my mind of Catherine sitting on the table in the doctor's office, fearfully squeezing my hand. I shook it away. If keeping her, and our child, healthy and safe meant that I had to keep my dick in my pants until the baby came, fine. We both hated it—I knew Catherine was frustrated with me—but it was the right choice.

I looked over and saw Hutch Morrison and Kellan Thomas in deep conversation near the copper farmhouse sink. Tonight was supposed to be a casual home-cooked dinner for the wedding guests staying at Casa di Rosabela, but there was nothing casual about what was going on in my kitchen. I knew a lot about food and wine— about eating and drinking the best of it, about investing in restaurants and talented chefs, about making wine—but even I was a little awed that two of the world's greatest culinary masters were in my home, sipping beers, swapping stories, and clearly enjoying the hell out of catching up. This was my kitchen, but there was no doubt that Kellan and Morrison were the masters of this domain.

Kellan had planned the menu. He'd recently returned from Italy, so the dishes were heavily influenced by spring in Tuscany. Morrison had been charged with sourcing the fresh ingredients this morning and he'd done a pretty amazing job. He was manning the lamb chops on the grill while Beckett and I were acting as the prep cooks, slicing and dicing under the chefs' watchful eyes.

I was no slouch in the kitchen, but next to these guys I felt like the amateur I was and I was taking my fair share of ribbing on my technique. No matter how much Morrison chided me about my sorry knife skills or how much Kellan egged me on for not chopping fast enough—for the amusement of our audience sitting at the kitchen table, I was sure—I was taking it all in stride.

"Finally," Kellan said in a mock-exasperated tone when I handed him the cutting board of the wild ramps I'd cleaned and separated. He looked over my work. "No blood or fingertips. That's a start."

I looked down at my hands, which were a little stained from the leafy green tops of the ramps. "All ten accounted for, Chef. Bring on the artichokes."

"I don't know. You might be a little rough yet, even for artichokes."

Everyone in earshot laughed at his quip, and I lifted my glass of wine to toast him. Normally, I wouldn't take that kind of shit from anybody, but tonight I was happy to laugh it off and cede to Kellan's expertise. I looked over at Catherine, her green eyes shining as she laughed at the teasing I was being subjected to. *Don't think that I'll let him get away with much more of that, beautiful girl*, I thought. A king could only take so much in his own castle.

Kellan Thomas wasn't as edgy as Morrison and he had about twenty years on both of us. Tonight, he was relaxed and playful, but he was still a demanding prick and I respected that about him. A man with seven Michelin stars to his credit had to be a prick and he was in a class by himself. His demand for perfection—from himself and from those who worked for him—was almost mythical. I'd eaten at Oro in Calistoga more times than I could count, and it never failed to be spectacular. Hell, I'd tried to imitate his dishes on more than one occasion and always came up woefully short.

Kellan motioned for me to step over to the range, so I set down my wine glass and walked over.

"Think a wooden spoon might be more your speed, Will." He handed me the overly long wooden spoon and pointed to the large copper pot simmering on the stove. "Stir. Until I tell you to stop. Twenty minutes or so—put all those muscles to good use."

I could smell the rich aroma of the lemon and pea risotto as I neared the bubbling pot. "Got it," I said, ignoring that he had called me 'Will.' "Why don't you grab a seat at the table with the ladies? A man your age should rest when he can."

"Fuck you, Lambourne," he chortled.

"Fuck you too. *Chef*."

I'd made my point. Kellan slapped me on the back, then

turned and grabbed his beer. He pulled a long sip from the bottle, then looked at me. "I think I'll try a glass of that rosé of yours I've heard so much about. All good things. I'm impressed. Can you spare a few cases for Oro?

I tried to keep a straight face. "I think I can manage to send a few cases your way. I'll call your sommelier next week."

"Excellent. Now keeping stirring." He walked away and I went back to making sure the Arborio rice wasn't sticking to the sides of the pot.

Getting a WML vintage into any Kellan Thomas restaurant would be a huge coup. We both knew it. Prick or not, he'd just opened a big ass door for me and I wouldn't forget his generosity.

SEVEN

Since all I had to focus on was the risotto, I glanced at the eating area where the guests were clustered around the big farm table. Kellan had brought his wife Electra, and she stood beside Catherine. Catherine wasn't short, but Electra had been a model, and she had height in spades, plus an exotic look that drew any red-blooded male's attention. Alec and Zoe were seated across from Catherine, and they were laughing and pouring more wine and offering a glass to Kellan. Electra offered her glass for a refill and, as she took a sip, gave me a thumb's up. I knew my rosé was good, but I still flushed with pride whenever someone gave my wine a stamp of approval.

I caught Catherine's gaze. She was sticking to mineral water tonight, but her wide eyes and big smile let me know she'd seen Electra's thumbs up, too. She knew how much the vineyard meant to me, and she shared my enthusiasm.

I don't know how I managed to get so fucking lucky. Catherine was gorgeous, smart, talented, sexy as hell, and she was all mine, heart and soul. She looked so *ripe* now, it was making me crazy. Every soft curve of hers was just a little more pronounced and when she walked into a room, I wanted to pin her against the wall, pull her legs up around my waist, and plunge myself into her. I was barely keeping myself in check and I wasn't sure how much longer I could keep my hands off of her.

"Lambourne, you stirring or blowing kisses to your fiancée?"

I gave Morrison the finger—again—and got back to work. I wasn't used to being the least accomplished man in the room, but I refused to give Morrison the satisfaction of me screwing up the risotto. He was a lot more personable than Kellan, but that didn't mean I liked him.

I'd backed many chefs when they'd opened restaurants in Chicago, but Morrison had never sought my help. He was an impressive chef, I'd give him that, and he'd made Morrison Hotel a huge success all on his own. But I still didn't trust the pretty bastard as far as I could kick his tattooed ass across my kitchen.

Catherine was always saying he and I could become great friends and pointed out all the ways we were alike—which never failed to piss me off. *She* was what we had in common, and I'd seen him openly admiring what was mine a few too many times. We would never be friends. But he was a part of Catherine's life whether I liked it or not, so I continued to make an effort. For her. It was important to her that we got along, so I did my best keep up the illusion.

I guess this is what people meant when they talked about putting someone else first. I never thought I'd meet a woman who would so wholly consume me from the moment we collided. I never thought I'd want to get married and I sure as hell never let myself dream of having a family. Yet now all of it was laid out before me, all because of her. If she hadn't supported me, I wouldn't have had the balls to start dismantling WML Capital Management and focus on the vineyard. Besides pursuing Catherine, that was the best decision I'd ever made.

There were days—too many days—when my tie had felt like a rope around my neck. From the outside, it looked like I ran the world, but the truth was WML Capital Management had run me. I'd been a slave to the schedule, to the demands, to the deadlines, and to a business I never really wanted to be in. I never got off on *the thrill of the deal* and making my money make more money proved almost too easy. But I'd done it for nearly a decade because it had been expected of me. I was William Lambourne III, anointed to take over my namesake's company since the moment his time had been cut short.

Fuck expectations. It took me nearly 20 years to figure that one out.

The vineyard had been a hobby at first, but Catherine had helped me realize that my life was happening *now* and I owed it to myself to pursue what *I* wanted. And that was to make wine. At the vineyard, I was building something from the ground up and I didn't answer to anyone. I did what I wanted, when I wanted. My MBA and years of experience in the business world helped, but I was also a farmer now, and a vintner, faced with unpredictable variables that were outside of my control every day. I should have hated it—I was a man who loved control—and sometimes it drove me crazy. But it was also everything I'd ever wanted. With Catherine by my side, I finally felt like I was living a life of purpose. I'd never been happier.

The threats from Elin Erickson were gone, too, and that was another load off my shoulders. I'd never told Catherine how much the extortion threats weighed on me. She was smart, so I'm sure she'd guessed some of it, but she would never know how close she came to actually being hurt, how close I had come to actually losing her. The cops had found detailed plans on Elin's computer. If we hadn't caught that freaky bitch at The Webster, her next step would have been to stage a little accident for Catherine. When I'd learned that, I'd wanted to break Elin's scrawny little neck. That wasn't possible, so instead I was doing everything I could to make sure she would rot in a prison cell for the rest of her natural life.

Elin Erickson and her ugliness were contained, but the press had been unrelenting since the news of her arrest was leaked. My crisis management team was on it 24/7, but the reality was my money and prominence would always make me—and my family— some kind of a target. I hadn't mentioned this to Catherine, but since we arrived in Napa I'd taken care of things. George Graham, my head of security, was still in Chicago, but he'd overseen an upgrade to all of the security protocols at the estate and the vineyard. He was now making the same upgrades to all of my other properties. If someone tried to mess with my future wife or my unborn child, it would be over my dead body.

Nothing and no one would ever so much as touch a hair on her head and that went for our future children, too.

I made damn sure of that.

"How's that risotto coming, Lambourne?" Kellan asked. He

set down his wine and made his way back to my side at the range.

"It's thickening nicely, but not too thick."

"Want to keep stirring or start on the salad?"

"I'm ready for salad." I moved back to the counter, handing over the wooden spoon and giving the chef free reign at the stove. That risotto was his specialty and it would have made him itch not to be the one to finish it. Besides, working at the counter gave me more opportunity to watch Catherine.

And Zoe.

Something was definitely simmering between Zoe and Morrison. I'd caught her looking his way all evening. I didn't like the idea of them together, but Zoe would have my balls if I told her who she could and couldn't date. Of the three cousins I'd grown up with, Zoe was the one I was closest to. She was spoiled, arrogant, hardheaded, and one of the tenacious people I knew, but she was also surprisingly sensitive, unfailingly loyal, and probably the best friend I'd ever had. It had been a pipe dream to think Zoe and Catherine would have hit it off. To say the first few meetings had been strained was an understatement. But Zoe had always been fiercely protective of me, and she was just being true to form. I couldn't blame Catherine for not warming to her.

Zoe had also always been the one who could read me best. After I broke it off with Catherine, she'd told me point-blank that I was a total idiot and a complete asshole for the way I'd acted. I'd be lucky if Catherine ever spoke to me again. Then she told me to get my ass on a plane to Paris and tell Catherine the truth about how I felt. Most people never got a chance at true love or the kind of happiness I'd stupidly pushed away. If I didn't reach for that with both hands, Zoe had said I'd regret it the rest of my life.

She'd been right, of course.

I lined up the roasted beets, which were still warm from the oven, and began to slice them into wedges, the red juice staining my already-stained fingers. Concentrating on the task hid my wince when I thought about that last day at the penthouse and how much of a dick I'd been to Catherine. The worst had been when she'd started sobbing and tried to kiss me. I hadn't been able to allow myself to respond and denying her had almost killed me. But I'd been convinced she'd be better off without me.

Zoe had been right to call me an idiot and an asshole. I'd been all that and more. But as any successful entrepreneur knew, it wasn't the successes that defined you but the failures. I never wanted to see Catherine in that kind of pain again, which is why I intended to spend the rest of my life making up for all the times I'd come up short with her. And *Mrs. Lambourne* sure had a nice ring to it.

I started mixing the ingredients for the balsamic vinaigrette, ducking when Beckett threw a block of Parmigiano-Reggiano over my head to Morrison.

"Sorry, man," Morrison said with a smile that said he was anything but sorry. "I promise to give you a head's up when the knives start flying."

At the table, Zoe poured another glass of wine for herself. When she caught me watching, she stuck her tongue out at me. With a laugh, I went back to mixing and whisking.

Zoe could hold her own. I knew that. That was one of the reasons I'd allowed her to get more involved in the Lambourne Foundation. There wasn't any way I could keep heading that up and spend the time I wanted with my soon-to-be-wife and the mother of my child. I felt surprisingly okay with the whole change, even though I'd resisted the idea at first. Zoe had solid ideas, and she was wicked smart. She could be a ballbuster when she wanted but underneath it all she had a heart—all qualities that would serve her well at the Foundation. I'd never wanted to give up control before, but now it was a relief.

I caught Catherine's eyes, and her smile warmed me all the way to my toes. It was easy to give up control when it meant more time with the one person I really cared about.

EIGHT

Outside, it was a perfect night with a clear sky and a million stars. The distressed wood table near the pool was set for a casual dinner and I'd ordered lights strung up between the Japanese maples along the border of the seating area. The small bulbs cast a soft glow. Portable heaters were scattered about and a fire was burning brightly in the outdoor fireplace, helping to ward off the evening chill. The whole scene reminded me how much I loved entertaining. Good food, good wine, good friends. It felt right with Catherine here to share it.

She was the last of the group to walk out from the house, and she looked hot as always. She was wearing a silky white maxi dress the seemed to float around her. It had a halter neckline with a small slit in the front, just enough that I could make out the high curved tops of her swaying breasts as she walked. Her tits weren't hanging out, but the dress gave a clear hint of her lusciousness underneath and I felt my cock begin to stir.

While everyone else found seats, I pulled her into my arms. She always smelled so good—just like...Catherine. I nuzzled her neck, breathing in that sweet smell and allowing my hands to roam down to her rounded ass. I gently cupped her bottom as I pulled her toward me, knowing she'd feel the effect she was having on me.

"You look ravishing tonight, beautiful girl," I whispered in her ear. She shivered in response. I loved when she did that.

She smiled up at me, her face glowing in the flickering light. Nothing and no one had ever felt as right as Catherine felt in my arms. And no one had ever made me so hard, so fast. I fought the urge to throw her down on the chaise longue behind me, push up that flimsy skirt, and slide my tongue all over what was mine.

"We can go upstairs right now, if you want. I'm not really hungry," she said quietly, a knowing smile on her glossy, pouty lips. She'd shifted in my arms and her hips were tilted just enough so that she was pressing against my now raging hard-on.

Fuck, I had to get a grip. I leaned and kissed her on her forehead as I backed away, avoiding the look I knew I'd see cross her face. "And miss the meal of a lifetime? Come on, I know you're starving. Let's eat."

I discreetly adjusted myself as I took her hand and walked her over to the table. I pulled out the chair next to mine and seated her, then took my own seat

Zoe was sitting next to Catherine, which was unexpected. They'd gotten off to such a rough start that Catherine had thought her being here this weekend might be awkward, but Zoe was smiling at her and being pleasant for once.

"Would you like some bread, Catherine?" she asked, passing the basket containing the aromatic loaf Beckett had baked earlier.

"Thanks." Catherine flashed me a puzzled smile.

Bowls and platters holding the rustic Tuscan feast were making their way up and down the table. I dished up some of Kellan's thick spaghetti with ramps and pancetta and then passed it to Electra. Morrison was on Zoe's left and I watched as he served her from the bowl of pasta in front of him. I stifled my annoyance at the way he looked at her. Fuck, the guy never quit. As much as I wanted to, I wasn't going to ruin the night by laying Morrison out cold on the pool deck.

Once everyone had tried the food, Electra raised her glass. "I propose a toast."

We joined her, lifting our glasses.

"To the chefs—the sexiest and most talented guys I know."

"Hear, hear!" Zoe raised her glass.

"And to the happy couple," I added.

"Cheers!" Everyone cried and moved to clink glasses. Catherine reached to tap her glass against me, her breasts brushing against my shoulder as she did so.

"Beckett, this bread is fantastic," Kellan called from beside his wife.

Alec moaned from the other end of the table. "Don't stroke his ego. It only encourages him."

"Hey!" Beckett pointed a finger. "Just wait until you taste the pie I made for dessert. I won't hear complaining about my midnight cooking sessions then."

"Are you working on anything new?" Catherine asked.

Beckett launched into a description of a new cupcake he wanted to debut at Patisserie Le Clerc. Normally I'd be interested, but I noticed Catherine was only picking at her food. I'd seen her do that often lately, and it worried me. She was eating for two. This was no time to push food around on the plate.

I wasn't the only one who noticed. A couple of minutes later, Zoe asked, "You okay, Cat? You're not eating much."

Catherine gave her a wan smile. "I have a bit of a headache."

"A headache, huh?" Zoe smirked at me, and I glared at her from my seat at the head of the table. *Shut the fuck up*, I told her with my eyes.

I knew I shouldn't have broken my promise to Catherine and told Zoe about the pregnancy. I'd sworn Zoe to secrecy, but obviously the wine was affecting her and loosening her tongue.

In my defense, I'd only told Zoe because I was out of my head with worry. We could have lost the baby when Catherine's IUD was removed, and her pregnancy was still high risk. What if the baby didn't make it? What if I lost them both? Those dark thoughts crept in sometimes, no matter how much I resisted them.

I didn't want to worry Catherine any more than she already was, so I'd caved and told Zoe. It had helped. She'd calmed me down and told me this wasn't something I could control, and I had to accept it. Life came with risks, it was as simple as that. Her words had helped, for the moment. Whatever happened, Catherine and I would get through it together.

I would've been happier if we were getting through it all as husband and wife, however. If it had been up to me, Catherine and I would have come back from Paris already married. She'd said yes to my proposal and was wearing her engagement ring, but she didn't seem to want to talk about our wedding. Something was up with that, but hell if I knew what it was. I wanted to ask her about it, but I also didn't want to push and risk upsetting her. She'd lost her first husband and I knew marriage was a tricky thing with her.

I forked up more of the excellent pasta. "Good choice on the ramps, Kellan," I said. "Tender and delicious. The egg is a nice touch, too."

"Our mutual friend was pretty persuasive when it came to adding the poached quail egg. I'll have to try it at the restaurant."

"And you'll fucking thank me, too," Morrison drawled from across the table.

Mutual friend, my ass.

I looked over at Catherine and she smiled at me again. Just looking at her mouth turned me on. It was proving harder than I thought to be careful of her in the bedroom. She'd woken me this morning with that amazing blowjob, but I'd cooled things right back down as soon as my brain started working. I couldn't risk hurting her no matter how badly I wanted to fuck her senseless. I'd left her hot and pouting in our bed, then jerked off—twice—in the shower just two minutes later.

Catherine leaned forward to reach for the bread basket, and the motion caused her breasts to push up slightly so they were visible in the slit at the front her dress.

Fuuuuuckkk.

My cock twitched again as I imagined nibbling a path from her neck all the way down to her sweet, sweet center.

So much for my control.

NINE

Friday morning
Catherine

When I woke I had a vague memory of William kissing me goodbye in the early morning before heading out to the vineyard. I'd thought about getting up with him, but my body had felt so heavy and warm, I'd fallen back into a deep sleep.

Finally, at the reasonable hour of ten, I climbed out of bed, showered, and dressed in a white eyelet sundress with a short black cardigan. I'd pulled my hair back into a ponytail and wore a light dusting of makeup. I headed downstairs, feeling rested and healthy, and when I made it to the kitchen, I wasn't at all surprised to see Beckett in there baking again, this time with Fernanda at his side.

William's security staff—Asa, Anthony, Nancy, and Sam—were seated at the farm table, mugs of coffee in hand, and what looked like a typed itinerary before them. Hutch was standing at the kitchen's island, going over menus. I offered them all a wave and sidled up to Beckett.

"Hey, you." His hands were covered in flour so I gave him a sideways hug. "You're up early."

"Cakes to bake, people to marry."

"I thought today you were just practicing the marrying," Hutch drawled from a barstool at the other side of the island.

60

"That's right." Beckett aimed a floury finger at me. "Don't be late, maid of honor. It's your job to keep me calm and remind me what to do. That's why we're having a rehearsal."

"We're all in trouble now," Hutch said, lifting his coffee cup to hide his smile.

"Ass," I said good-naturedly. "Beckett, I've got your back."

"Are you nervous, Mr. Beckett?" Fernanda asked, her slight accent coming through. She was a petite, industrious woman who was dwarfed by Beckett's height.

"Not at all, 'Nanda," Beckett said with a wink. "I feel like I've been waiting for this forever."

"Aw, that's sweet," Hutch drawled. "We should all be so lucky."

I couldn't help but try to read between the lines of that last statement. Since when did Hutch want to get married?

"Miss Cat, can I make you something for breakfast? Some fruit?" Fernanda offered.

"Oh, no." Hutch stood. "I saved some of my signature chicory coffee and fresh beignets for her. I had to fight off those hungry ninjas over there to do it." He pointed to the table of security. Prim Nancy looked offended, but Anthony just lifted his beignet and toasted before taking a huge bite.

"I can't resist that offer," I said, vowing to drink just a few sips of the coffee, and keeping it to two beignets. I might be pregnant, but I still had a dress to squeeze into for tomorrow's ceremony. "Thanks, Hutch." I gave him a quick hug and took a deep breath. No matter whether he was in Paris, Chicago, or Napa, he always smelled smoky and exotic.

While Hutch fixed a plate for me and Fernanda insisted on adding a side of fresh fruit (if I let my paranoia get the better of me, I'd swear she knew about my delicate condition), Darius came in. He was another member of William's security team and was a big military-looking guy with a shaved head who always walked like he was late for a briefing at the Pentagon.

Darius eyed me warily. I didn't think he liked me much. I'd given him the slip in downtown St. Helena the last time I was here. I'd taken off with Jeremy Ryder right under his nose and he hadn't been able to stop me. I was sure he'd gotten all kinds of hell from William for that mistake and I was surprised William hadn't fired him.

"Miss Kelly," he said politely, nodding at me before going to the table full of security personnel. He and Sam spoke briefly and then the two of them marched off. Interesting pair, I thought as I watched Sam, who was older, slimmer, and had that awful grey ponytail, keep step with the imposing Darius.

I took the barstool beside the one Hutch had been occupying and admired the view of the vineyards behind Beckett. It was another beautiful day, and everyone seemed to be in a good mood, anticipating the events of the afternoon.

"It's not breakfast in bed," Hutch said, "but since Lambourne would kick my ass if I tried to get near your bed, it will have to do."

I rolled my eyes and bit into a warm beignet. My stomach

felt surprisingly settled this morning, and I was even a little hungry. Maybe I truly was past the first trimester morning sickness, or maybe my little *lime* was giving me a break because he knew how much I wanted these beignets. I'd found a chart online, which conveniently matched the size of a baby to a fruit of roughly the same size for each gestational week. I photographed food for a living, so I understood the scale of fruit.

"I have a surprise for you, Kitty Cat." Hutch gestured to his tablet on the island before us, swiping a finger across it to wake it up.

"More naked pictures of you? I told you to stop sending those."

Beckett snorted.

"Very funny, darlin'. Trust me, if I sent you naked pictures, you wouldn't be telling me to stop."

He was probably right. He wore his usual tight jeans and black T-shirt, both of which showed off his very toned, very muscled physique. The edges of tattoos peeked out from the sleeves of his T-shirt, and I couldn't help but stare. I'd always wondered where else he hid his ink.

"These are the digital galleys for the e-cookbook. Galleys are—"

"Layouts for you to proof. I know." I leaned forward over Hutch's tablet, eager to get a glimpse of the project I'd worked so hard on. I wanted to go straight to the photos, but I ended up lingering a bit on some of the prose. Though I knew he worked with an editor, Hutch had a terrific writing style. It was easy and charming, just like the man.

Finally, I swiped through photos of Tasso pork tenderloin with goat cheese grits, smoked tomato and morel medley, and even shots of brown sugar beignets with blueberry compote and chicory coffee like I was enjoying now. The pictures seemed to leap off the screen, the colors vibrant and alive, and the food looked downright sexy, just like Hutch had wanted.

"You're pretty fucking talented," Hutch said, sipping his coffee.

"I am. I really am." I gave him a smile, but he didn't smile back. He nodded at me with a look in his eye that made me think *uh-oh. Here it comes.*

"So why haven't you called Pierre Manon or James Benson back? I know they both want to book you for a few shoots."

I shrugged and tried to act casual. "If you hadn't noticed, I'm busy with my maid of honor duties." I made a point to sound light and casual, hoping my voice didn't betray the real reason I had commitment issues at work. I waved as Asa and Anthony headed out the door. Behind us, Nancy chirped brightly on her cell about arrival times and staging locations.

"I'm sure you have enough time to make a few phone calls. Catherine"—Hutch took my hand—"I didn't hire you to shoot my cookbook because you have a pretty face and a killer body. That didn't hurt but—"

"Hutch," I warned.

"My point is I hired you because I'd seen your work. You

have a real gift, one that more people should see. I don't know if you don't believe how talented you are...."

"I do believe in myself." I cut him off and gave his hand a pat as I removed mine from his grip.

"Well then, I hope it's not that diamond that's keeping you from work."

"Hutch!" I tried my best to sound offended, when really I was shocked that Hutch was so spot-on. The diamond was absolutely responsible, though not literally, of course. "I appreciate you opening so many doors for me, I truly do. I'll call Manon and Benson as soon as I get a chance. I promise." I had no idea whether that would be to accept or reject the offers, though. Everything was so in flux at the moment that work had taken a back seat. But looking at these pictures it was impossible not to want to get back behind my camera.

Out of nowhere, I felt tears beginning to well up in my eyes—hormones again, damn it. I missed working, yet I was ignoring work. And my art. Where *was* I these days? I didn't have a darkroom at Casa di Rosabela, though I was sure if I told William I wanted one, he'd build one right away. But I hadn't really felt like working on my personal photography projects these past two weeks, either. Because I was on vacation—but I wasn't really on vacation.

I realized Hutch was staring at me, which snapped me back into the moment. I tried to think how to appease him before he thought my tears were because he was my white knight and I was *tearfully* grateful for all that he was doing for me. He could be single-minded when he wanted something, and he was beginning to get that look in his eyes.

"Why don't I call them for you and set something up? I'd even be willing to go with you to a meeting," Hutch said softly. Too late; he'd obviously seen my eyes well and now was trying to be sweet.

Zoe, coffee in hand, chimed in to my rescue. "Why does Catherine need you to go to a meeting with her?" she asked, pushing her way in as usual. She leaned a hip on the island, angling herself so she could see Hutch and me.

"Good morning to you, too, darlin'."

"He doesn't need to go to a meeting with me," I told Zoe. "Hutch, you don't have to hold my hand. I promise, I'll follow up on those offers as soon as…" As soon as what? When was all of this going to feel real?

"Hell, no." Hutch waved a hand. "You have to be decisive. You have too much talent to dither around."

"Dither?" I asked, trying desperately to change topics. "What does *dither* mean?"

"All right, smart ass. You have too much talent to *fuck* around. You gotta take these opportunities and run with them."

"Hey, Morrison," Zoe interrupted "Take a breath, okay?"

To my amazement, Hutch actually did what she said.

"You made your case, and it's solid. Let her make her own decision. She's a smart woman. She knows what she's doing."

I did? Zoe thought I was smart? I looked at her. If I was, I wasn't smart enough to figure out why she was helping me.

Hutch narrowed his eyes. "She is smart, which is why I don—"

"I was thinking about taking a walk through the olive grove." Zoe set her coffee on the island. "Want to join me?"

Hutch's expression was torn for a moment. Part of him obviously wanted to keep pushing at me, but another part of him seemed to want very much to take Zoe up on her offer of a walk. Finally, his sex drive or whatever won, and he gave Zoe a nod. "Sure, I'll join you." He rose, but before Zoe could pull him out he pointed at me. "Think about what I said, you got that, Kitty Cat?"

"Yes, sir."

Zoe took his arm and led him toward the door, smiling at me over her shoulder. Weird. It was almost like she was trying to help me. I was glad she did because I was running out of excuses.

I took a deep breath and ate another beignet before focusing back on Beckett. "So, as requested, no bachelorette party, but I booked an appointment at that fabulous spa in St. Helena."

"Cat, I told you that wasn't necessary." Beckett had two tiers of cake set on top of each other, and he was trying to make sure the edges were even.

"I'm the maid of honor. Of course it's necessary!"

"You've already provided a gorgeous venue and world-renowned chefs. I think you're off the hook. Besides"—he gave me a sheepish look—"I promised Alec we'd spend some time alone before the rehearsal. William said we could borrow one of his cars and hit a few wineries."

That actually sounded like a really lovely idea. I could totally see Beckett and Alec cruising around the golden countryside in a convertible, just holding hands and enjoying some wine tastings before their big day.

"But you should totally go to the spa, Cat."

"Maybe I will."

"Are you mad?" Beckett asked.

"No! If I wasn't such a good maid of honor, I'd insist on chaperoning you and Alec because your plan sounds greats"

"Thanks."

"So I guess I have no official duties until the rehearsal." I was not only the maid of honor but the main wedding photographer, although I had an assistant coming in later to help with some of the shots because I couldn't shoot pictures if I was in them.

Hutch had left his tablet on the island, and I scrolled through more of the cookbook pages. Just looking at the shots made me itch to have my Leica in my hand. "If you don't need me, I think I'm going to grab my camera and wander around."

Beckett waved a hand. "Go and shoot photos. You'd probably like that more than the spa anyway."

He was right, of course.

TEN

Through the lens of my Leica, the wine cave looked incredible in the late morning light. I hadn't touched this camera much in recent weeks and it felt good to have it back in my hands. William and I had chatted about adding some shots of the vineyard to the marketing campaign for WML Champagne, so I decided to start getting a feel for how the vineyard would photograph.

The cave's arched wooden doors were probably ten feet high and surrounded by vines. The sunlight hit at just the right angle so that the vines' shadows made beautiful patterns on the old doors. Otherwise, the cave was pretty unremarkable from the outside. Just a slight stone rise nestled into a hillside covered by neatly kept rows of grapes.

The huge doors served not only to enlarge the entrance and allow small loading vehicles in and out, but, as William had explained to me, to seal the cave off and keep the temperature optimum and the humidity in. I gave the left door a tug and it opened easily.

I bypassed the workroom with its wooden workbenches and then the formal tasting room with its elegant area rugs and groupings of tables and chairs and headed down and deeper into the cave. It was chilly and dark, the soft lighting strung along the high rounded stone ceilings illuminating row after row of bottle-filled racks as well as barrels of wine. The huge aluminum vats that held William's reserves for his champagne lined one wall and I took a few shots to test the lighting. I was worried it would be too dark to get a good shot, but the dim light made the place look romantic and atmospheric.

The cave was mostly silent with an occasional creak or groan from one of the barrels or the racks of bottles. I wasn't afraid, though. In fact, I'd stopped looking over my shoulder ever since Elin had been caught and put in jail. The wine cave held a huge amount of valuable liquid inventory and William had state of the art security everywhere. This place was as secure as Fort Knox—probably even more so.

I continued walking, the clicking of my shoes echoing off of the vaulted walls, until I reached where William's special vintages of sparkling wine were aged. More rows of bottles greeted me, but these bottles were almost upside down. I'd learned from William that making sparkling wine by the traditional *method champagnoise* was crazy complicated and someone had to turn each and every one of these bottles just a little bit every day. It was called riddling and if this important step in the process was overlooked, the wine would be ruined.

William had a few riddlers in his employ, which I thought was hilarious. "Do they tell you jokes while they're turning the bottles? Maybe you can learn something from them," I'd sassed to him when he finally took me on my first tour of the cave. William excelled at just about everything, but telling jokes was one thing he didn't do well. "It's a serious job," he'd answered, but he hadn't quite been able to keep the corner of his mouth from turning up. But I didn't see Vincent or Joseph this morning, so I was alone for now.

The solitude and peace of the cave were a welcome relief. With the constant deliveries of linens, chairs, and serving items, the house and grounds had been noisy and full of people walking purposefully, phones in hand. It was nice to have time to think and escape all the hustle and bustle until later.

I strolled between the rows, reminded of the champagne shoot Beckett and I had worked on. William had wanted what I liked to call a "champagne orgasm shot," and it had taken some research and special effects. The shoot had been fun, but the memory was marred for me—that was the day we'd found out about Elin and had made that awful trip to the Cook County Jail. It had been the beginning of the end really, since Will had started to pull away from me then and had broken my heart the very next day. Despite all that, the pictures from the champagne shoot had turned out really great. And now here I was, ready to take more shots of champagne in William's gorgeous wine cave.

Everywhere I looked, I could see his hand—the organization, the labels on the bottles, the myriad of other details. He'd transformed this place into what I knew would be a hugely successful vineyard that put out highly rated products. I was so proud of him. He'd made his dream come true, and the cave, the grapes, the bubbly champagne were all his. I could almost hear William correcting me. He'd say it was all ours, but I'd never get used to that idea.

I heard a footstep behind me and turned to see the man himself. He was smiling at me from the workroom, and my belly did a slow roll that had nothing to do with the baby or morning sickness. My body still reacted every time I saw him. My legs weakened, my breath shortened, and heat rushed into my core. I wondered if I would ever get used to him, if my need for him would ever diminish from blaze to low simmer.

With a smile, I walked toward him and eyed the large purple grapes in his hand. "Did you pick those?"

I slid along the nearby table and stood before him, putting my hands on his waist. Even in the soft light of the cave, I could tell his eyes had turned the soft molten grey of arousal. He was still warm from being outside, and he smelled like a spring breeze, freshly turned earth, and William.

"No. These are a variety we're thinking about." He plucked one and held it to my lips. Obediently, I opened and bit down on the plump, ripe flesh. The grape was so ripe a bit of juice squirted on the side of my mouth. Before I could lick it away, William's finger slid over the liquid. He sucked on his finger, his gaze never leaving mine.

Heat and urgency surged through my body. I needed him like I needed water or air or sunlight. I grasped a fistful of his thick, dark curls and yanked his mouth to mine.

To my delight, William was as eager as I was. Finally. His thick tongue slid into my mouth, filling it. I tore at his hair, kissing him deeper and harder and pushing him back until I'd cornered him against a wall. He matched the thrusts of my tongue, his hands pulling me close until my breasts crushed against his chest. The contact felt *so* good. I rubbed against him and the friction left me breathless.

"Can you tell how much I want you?" I moaned into his mouth.

"Almost as much as I want you."

I heard the playful tone in his voice.

"I'm burning up." It was true. Every part of me felt hot and tender and his every touch stoked the inferno raging inside me.

"Is this what marriage to you will be like? Morning blowjobs and trysts in the wine cave?" He grasped my wrists as he swung me around until I was pushed against the wall. He raised my arms above my head and pressed his pelvis against me, his erection straining against the button-fly of his distressed jeans. He had me pinned against the cool stone and I loved the feeling of being captured by this big, muscular, very aroused man. We hadn't played like *this* in weeks

I bantered back breathlessly. "Probably. You want to call off the engagement?"

"Not a chance." His mouth took mine again, and he kissed me so long and so deeply that I was practically purring when he pulled away.

"Fuck, I want you so fucking much right now." The rawness in his voice sent a shot of heat through me and my arousal gushed between my legs. I wanted to beg him to strip off my soaked panties and touch me where I needed him.

"I want you, too. It's been too long. I'm going crazy without you inside me."

He groaned. "I *want* to be inside you. You don't know how much."

"Then what are you waiting for? Fuck me, William."

Another groan. "Catherine, I don't think—"

I put a finger over his lips. "That's the problem. You're thinking too much."

He shook his head. "Catherine…"

I silenced him with my mouth, showing him with my tongue what I wanted.

When he released my arms and we broke apart, we were both breathing hard. For the first time, his hands cupped my breasts, and I closed my eyes from the sheer blissful agony of it.

"You are so unbelievably sexy," he rasped right before he split open the little buttons on the bodice of my sundress. I wasn't wearing a bra because I didn't have any strapless ones that fit my new pregnant boobs, and he inhaled sharply at the sight of my bare flesh.

"Holy fuck. Your nipples are so pink. So swollen." His eyes were impossibly dark and desire seemed to radiate off of him as he eyed me hungrily.

"Touch me," I begged. "I need you to…"

I didn't even have a chance to finish before his hands cupped my breasts and his thumbs slid over my hard points. I was so sensitive that the slightest touch felt magnified a thousandfold.

"More," I moaned.

His mouth closed on one nipple, and I dug my nails into his shoulder because the feeling was the closest thing to an orgasm I'd felt in so long. William's hands and lips suckled and nuzzled until I was so turned on my vision dimmed.

"I want to taste you." He cupped my sex, and the world seemed to tilt.

"Please, I want you inside me." I reached my hand down and stroked his thick erection through his jeans.

The sound he made was like an animal in pain, but he didn't release the buttons on his fly. Instead, he gripped me by the waist and shifted me to on top of an empty oak cask. I didn't want to sit. I wanted him to take me against the wall or push me onto the floor, but before I could argue, he flipped my skirt up and yanked my panties down.

"Stay still, beautiful girl. You are very wet for me, aren't you?" he said.

"Uh huh," I breathed as I wiggled my hips and lifted my bottom as he pulled my saturated lilac lace panties down my thighs.

The slow slide of the fabric down my legs was torture and I was quivering and swollen and ready to tip over the edge. "Hurry, William. Please...I can't..."

At that, William growled then ripped my panties and stuffed them in his pocket. He shoved my legs apart and then his mouth was on that pulsing, needy part of me.

The first orgasm hit me right away and I screamed. My hips

bucked, but his tongue didn't cease its slow, measured torment of my slick sex.

"God, you taste good," he murmured against my thigh. I could feel my moisture on his chin.

I leaned back, bracing my hands on the rim of the cask, thrusting my breasts up and spreading my legs.

"I want you inside me, William."

I meant his cock, but he dipped his tongue into my slit and I almost rose off the cask. He followed a rhythm my body reveled in: tongue deep inside, then a slide through my folds, a flick over my clit, and then back inside my opening. I was practically crying from need. And just when I was about come again, he withdrew.

"Don't stop," I panted

"I won't, but just be patient." He reached for a bottle of champagne on a rack nearby, popped the cork with an efficiency I could appreciate, and then poured the frothy liquid all over my exposed breasts.

"William!" I squealed at the coldness of the champagne. My nipples reacted instantly and pulled into tight, hard points. And then he was touching me again, with his hands and then with his tongue, kneading my aching breasts. I wanted to cry.

"You are so fucking beautiful like this, Catherine," he said, his voice low and reverent, "so flushed, so full. Your breasts look amazing coated in my champagne,"

"Mm hmm," I moaned. I was pure sensation, sparks shooting from each place on my body he touched. Then his finger slid down to circle my clit as he splashed champagne over my thighs. The cool liquid dribbled over my opening, and I clenched with need. William's tongue lapped up the sweet evanescence and I couldn't stop my hips from moving, from riding that tongue until I shattered again.

"Now." I reached for him when I'd come down and could think again. "I want you inside me."

"You're insatiable." He spread my knees and opened me again. I wanted to argue, to *demand* his cock, but his tongue was so skilled, and he was so patient, bringing me right to the edge of another climax and then edging back again. I was delirious with desire, and it was all I could do not to fall off the cask. I draped my legs over her shoulder, urging him deeper, thrusting with him, begging him to make me come.

And when he did, for the third time, I fell forward so he caught me in his arms. I was spent, well and truly spent, and yet I still felt the absence of penetration. No fingers inside me. No big thick cock. As much pleasure as his tongue gave me, I wanted more.

I was still vaguely aroused, and I wondered if maybe he was right and I was becoming insatiable. If I couldn't have his hard cock inside my body, maybe I could take it inside my mouth.

I stroked the bulge in his jeans again. "Should I return the favor?" I slid the button through the hole.

"I was hoping you'd offer."

I took the second button between two fingers.

"Mr. Lambourne? Are you in here?" A masculine voice

called from several feet down the corridor.

"Shit." William rose and moved to block me from view. "Yes. I'll be out in a moment." His voice echoed while his deft fingers fastened his jeans again.

"Just a couple of questions, sir." The voice called again.

"Give me one minute."

William put his hands around my waist and lifted me from my seat atop the cask. The skirt of my white eyelet sundress fluttered down as he righted me on my feet, though I was now without panties. My legs felt wobbly and I swayed against him.

He looked me up and down and then began to button up the bodice of my dress. I stood there like a child as his big fingers fumbled with the delicate little buttons. "We can't have you walking out of here all undone now, can we?"

I giggled. "You're my undoing, William. Thank you." I leaned in and gave him a gentle kiss. My red hot lover was coming back to me, I knew it, and I felt almost giddy with relief.

"Anytime, beauty." He shifted again and struggled to adjust himself. I could see that he was still hard.

"Looks like you're the frustrated one now. This"—I gestured to his erection—"is how I've felt for the past week and a half at least."

He ran his fingers across my lips. "Oh, we're not finished, Catherine. Not by a long shot. "

ELEVEN

Friday evening
William

The afternoon had been busier than expected, which meant I hadn't gotten back to Catherine as I'd intended. I'd had her taste on my tongue all day, could still feel the weight of her amazing tits in my hands, but mitigating shipping issues with our vendors and a half dozen phone calls had kept me from finding her and fucking her on the spot. That, and remembering that going after her like a rutting fucking stallion probably wasn't a good idea.

I'd just showered and dressed and was making my way through the house and to the dining room, letting the battle play out in my head. Beckett and Alec's rehearsal dinner was tonight so Catherine would be busy. As much as I shouldn't, maybe I'd convince her to slip away for a while so we could finish what we'd started in the wine cave. I wanted to see those swollen tits again. I wanted to tongue those hard nipples and then bury my face in her sweet, sweet pussy.

I hadn't seen any worry in Catherine's eyes this afternoon, only hot longing. She'd practically begged for my cock and seemed to think there was no reason for us to abstain. I still sensed that there were things she wasn't telling me—but she was acting more like her old self. Did I need to continue keeping my distance? Hell if I knew anymore.

And I was going to be hard again if I didn't stop thinking about her. I could hear the murmur of voices and the clink of silver on china. I took a deep breath and rounded the corner into the dining room that opened onto to the terrace.

God damn it, I muttered as soon as I stepped inside. I knew instantly there would no sneaking away. The dining room was massive and Beckett didn't have a huge guest list, but there were enough guests to fill the space comfortably. Catherine was in the center of it all, holding court and effortlessly introducing people and making certain they had drinks and felt welcome. I could have stood and watched her for hours. I'd always known she would fit perfectly into my life, but I couldn't believe how it seemed she had always been a part of this house and everything in it. She was a flawless hostess.

Last night she'd looked flirty and sexy, but tonight she was elegant and sexy in a black sleeveless dress with semi-sheer lace that started mid-thigh and dropped to the floor. The skirt silhouetted her long, lithe legs and her sexy high heels. An image of those legs wrapped around my waist, her stilettos digging into my ass as I plowed into her dripping center flashed in my head. I coughed, willing the X-rated images away as I kept admiring my fiancée.

Her coppery hair was pulled into a loose bun and the plunging neckline of the dress showed off her gorgeous cleavage and long neck. I would have liked to circle that expanse of flesh in a collar of diamonds, but I knew she'd reject a lavish gift like that as too much. The engagement ring on her left hand, which caught the light and sparkled as she chatted animatedly with a guest, was indication enough—for now, at least—that she was taken, that she was mine.

The guy she was talking to was olive skinned, muscular, and heavily tattooed. He'd dressed all in black and wore a black porkpie hat. The way he was eyeing her told me he was into her and intent on what she was saying. Why wouldn't he be? She was a knockout in that dress, showing just enough skin to make any man want to see more.

Hipster Guy moved in and whispered something close to Catherine's ear, and I felt the hair on the back of my neck prickle. My fists clenched involuntarily, and I blew out a breath instead of marching over there and ripping his head off. I got myself in check before I took slow, measured steps toward them.

As usual, Catherine sensed I was close and looked up to lock eyes with me. One look from her calmed me instantly, but inflamed me, too. The desire in her eyes was for me alone, just like I wanted. She motioned me over and I was able to nod at Hipster Guy semi-politely.

"William, I'd like introduce you to Alejandro Vargas." She gestured to Hipster Guy with one slim hand. "He's creating tonight's dinner with Hutch and Kellan."

Morrison's lackey. I should have known.

I stuck out my hand and Vargas took it. Good handshake, not

too tight and solid.

"Alejandro was just telling me about his trip to Point Reyes this morning to pick up oysters. It was eventful, apparently." She smiled at Vargas and then me, her green eyes shining and her face radiant. She looked so happy that I couldn't help but smile back. Man, every time I saw her I couldn't stop thinking about how fucking lucky I was.

"Nice to meet you, Mr. Vargas," I said. "Welcome. How is it that Morrison let you out of the kitchen? Not that we mind, of course." I said the last for Catherine, who smiled at us both.

Vargas laughed. "Morrison is an alright dude, but I work for Kellan. I'm his *poissoinier*."

Catherine furrowed her brow.

"You know, his fish guy," Vargas continued. "I'm also the saucier for tonight. I was just asking Catherine here where to find more ice and when I mentioned the oysters, she said you'd changed her mind about them. Pretty recently, right?"

She nodded with a quick look at me. Her eyes were sparkling and I knew she was thinking of our sexy dinner a few months ago, the one where I'd blindfolded her with my tie and hand-fed her. She'd said she hated oysters, but then sampled the warm oysters with champagne sabayon I'd prepared and became a fan. I'd used that same tie to bind her wrists together before I fucked her later that night and she'd become a fan of that, too.

Fuck, I swear she was trying to kill me. I drifted back to the conversation. Vargas was talking.

"And then I mentioned Point Reyes, and we started talking surfing. I can't believe you're Jace Ryder's wife." He nodded to Catherine. I felt my whole body stiffen.

"I mean, *was* his wife. I idolized that dude when I was in high school. He could pull off a perfect roundhouse cutback on a two-foot swell with his eyes closed. He was that incredible."

I kept my smile plastered on my face. I didn't want Catherine to see how awkward the whole conversation felt to me. But kudos to Vargas for having the class not to mention the accident that had killed Jace, the accident I knew Catherine would always feel responsible for.

Catherine had a life before me and I had a life before her. But her past life just happened to be that of the fearless photographer wife of a famous world-class surfer. There were some dark episodes there, too, and Elin Erickson had done her best to remind the world of those not very long ago. I didn't give a shit about what had happened years ago, but Catherine had been beside herself and there was nothing I could do to take away that hurt. Sometimes I wasn't sure if she'd ever let go of the past and I hated that it had the power to unnerve me.

But she was mine now.

That was all that mattered.

She was mine.

I felt Catherine's warm fingers against my knuckles, and she slipped her hand into mine. It was like she could sense my conflicted emotions and knew I needed her reassurance and she mine.

I cleared my throat. "I never saw Jace surf, but I've heard he was very talented. Catherine's told me, and I've seen her photos, of course. And you, Mr. Vargas, I've long admired your work. I had a poached flounder with mint *beurre blanc* when I dined at Oro a few months ago. It was as close to perfection on a plate as I've ever eaten. I suspect you had something to do with that."

"I might have," Vargas answered, his big smile evidence that he appreciated the compliment.

"The mint was an ingenious addition. Interesting flavor profile."

"Yeah. You know, that was kind of an accident." Vargas told us how he'd come to decide to add mint to the sauce, and while normally I'd be interested, I was distracted by the sensation of Catherine's skin as I rubbed my thumb over her palm.

Finally Vargas excused himself to fetch more ice and take it to the kitchen and the oysters, and I made my move.

"I need to talk to you for a minute." I didn't wait for her to respond, and I didn't care if our absence would be noticed. I was already holding her hand, so I pulled her through the crowd. It took a lifetime to get through the guests—all the hellos and other bullshit—but I finally led her through the open doors and down the hall toward my study. I knew it was empty.

Once inside, I closed the door, then shoved her up against it, keeping her exactly where I wanted her. I had to put my mouth on those sweet lips of hers, but when I kissed her, it was anything but sweet. She always made me want to go deeper, harder, hotter. Her hands ran up my arms, distracting me, and when I grasped her wrists and raised them above her head, pinning them to the door, she groaned aloud. I loved how she responded when I restricted her movement, how she responded to my taking control, and tonight, the position made the fabric of her dress dip down over her breasts, so I had a clear view of rounded breasts spilling out of her lacy black bra.

"You are making me crazy tonight, beautiful girl," I growled as I moved so my throbbing cock pressed against her, against all her softness and luscious curves. I couldn't get enough of her. I wanted to kiss every inch of her, breathe her in, and claim she was *mine, mine, mine.*

I nudged her chin up with my nose and pressed my lips against that soft part of her neck that was always so sensitive. When she gave a little mewl of pleasure, I almost lost it right there. Sometimes she made me feel like I was seventeen again.

I trailed back to her lips, taking my time to kiss every inch of her, and her mouth met mine eagerly. Her tongue danced with mine, drawing me into her and then following me. Finally, I pulled back to look at her.

Her cheeks were pink, her lips swollen, and I liked seeing my hands on her wrists against the door. She looked delicious, and I was hungry for more.

"We'd better get back to our guests," she cooed. She had that little smile on her lips that made me crazy. Fuck. I wanted her so bad.

"They can wait." I couldn't. I pushed my hips forward, making sure she could feel how much I wanted her.

She moaned with pleasure at the contact, and I felt the heat of her pressed against me. Suddenly I closed my eyes, struggling for control. What the fuck was I doing? I had a house full of guests just steps away, but *fuck*. All I could think about was ripping her panties off and plunging as deep into her warm wetness as I could. The wine cave was the first time I'd had my mouth on her since Paris all those weeks ago and now she was the like the oasis to my desert thirst and I was dying for another drink.

Reluctantly, I released her hands and pulled her into my lap as I sat us down on the leather arm chair near the door. We were both breathing hard and a few tendrils of her hair had come loose and frame her face. She probably wanted to go back to the party, but I wasn't ready to release her yet.

Surprisingly, she didn't say a word as I settled us into the chair and positioned her where I wanted. It wasn't as close a connection as I needed after Alejandro Hipster Vargas and all the talk about Jace, but I knew by now Catherine was my woman. But I had to get my shit together. We had guests waiting, and if I was going to throw caution to the wind, it wasn't going to be for a quick fuck up against a wall in the middle of a party. I wanted her slow and thorough and in my bed. In *our* bed.

I resigned myself to kissing her and fondling those amazing tits through her dress. "You look so elegant tonight," I told her. I grazed the knot she'd wrapped her long hair into and imagined taking it down. "You always look so beautiful."

"So do you," she murmured. "I love you, William."

I never got tired of hearing that.

"I love you, too, Catherine." And then I kissed her until neither of us could breathe just to prove it.

"Really," she said when we both came up for air. "Everyone will be wondering where we are." Her voice, even frustrated, was like a caress.

"Yeah, you're probably right. Let's get back to the guests, beautiful girl." I rose from the couch, not yet ready to let Catherine go. She was so light anyway that it was no real effort. Plus, I loved the feel of her against my chest.

Catherine squirmed. "Put me down, please. You don't have to carry me!"

"It's all I want to do," I told her. "You know that. I love to carry you and I can't wait to carry my *wife* across the threshold." My chest felt warm as soon as the words were out. I knew why. The words were important. They were all I really wanted—to marry Catherine.

"William…" Catherine's voice trailed off, and her expression was suddenly serious. I let her go, and she slid to her feet. "You know it's not that easy. Plus we can't talk about it now. Come on, let's go back to the party. Dinner is going to be served soon. We can't miss that."

I clenched my jaw. I was right, she was avoiding something. And why the fuck was she hesitating??

I'd learned to be patient with her and for the moment, the subject of our marriage was off limits.

For the *moment*.

I gestured to the door. "Lead the way, baby."

TWELVE

Almost as soon as we returned to the dining room, a woman with long blond hair and hazel eyes grabbed Catherine and hugged her. "Cat, it's been forever," she squealed—or perhaps the squealing came from Catherine—as the women embraced. "I can't believe my little brother is getting married."

I realized this must be Beckett's older sister, Lucia. I watched the two women try to figure out how long it had been since they'd last seen each other, and then Lucia turned to me. "And you must be William, right? I know we have you to thank for this amazing weekend, not to mention the smile on this girl's face."

I liked this woman already.

"Lucia." I held out my hand. "Nice to meet you. I hope your trip was uneventful."

"Ha! I'm traveling with a five-year-old. That's an event in itself."

Just then a boy with curly brown hair and blue eyes hugged his mother's leg. Lucia wrapped an arm around his shoulders. "This is Cole. Say hello to Mr. Lambourne, bug."

The kid gave me a smile that showed off one missing tooth before he stuck out his hand and said, "I'm Cole Douglas. How do you do?"

"A pleasure to meet you, Cole Douglas." I bent slightly and took his hand, shaking it. I couldn't help but compare this sweet kid with the image in my mind of our future son. Like Cole, maybe he'd have dark hair and possibly my blue eyes. If he took after Catherine, he'd charm the pants off everyone he met—just like Cole was doing.

"Do you have any toys?"

"Cole!" Lucia gave me an apologetic look.

"It's fine. I'm sure he's bored by the adult party." I glanced around and spotted Fernanda. She saw my wave and stepped out of the room, returning a moment later with a shopping bag. "I knew Cole would be here, so I took the liberty of picking up a few things that might keep him occupied."

"Here you go, *niño*." Fernanda handed the bag to Cole, who wasted no time pulling out the first Lego set. It was some kind of Star Wars spaceship.

"A T-16 Skyhopper. Cool!"

"Beckett said he liked Legos, and I figured every kid likes Star Wars," I told Lucia. I was playing it off, but secretly I was relieved that Cole liked the gifts.

"And an Imperial Troop Transport!" Cole yelled. "Awesome!"

Lucia pressed a hand to her heart. "Thank you, William. Cole, tell Mr. Lambourne thank you."

"Thank you!" Cole beamed at me.

"You're welcome. Why don't you take them inside with Fernanda? There's plenty of light there and space on the table off the kitchen."

"Can I, Mom?"

"Sure. I'll come with you to get you settled." Lucia started to walk toward the house, shepherding Cole in front of her as he determinedly held the shopping bag of Legos with two hands. Then she stopped abruptly, turned back, and looked at Catherine. "He *is* really something, Cat. I knew he'd have to be if he won you."

I turned to look at Catherine. Her eyes were watery and filled with emotion as she smiled back at Lucia. I'd be an idiot not to know she was thinking about us and what we would be like with our own kid. If we weren't at the fucking party, I would have pulled her aside and told her I was feeling the same thing. The future scared the hell out of me, but I was so excited for it, too.

I drew her toward me and wrapped my arm around her waist. She let out a little sniffle, so I pulled my handkerchief from my trouser pocket and handed it to her.

"Thank you," she said softly and I just nodded and smiled down at her. I didn't know what to say, and besides, I wasn't sure I could say anything without choking up.

Ever since Paris, I wasn't sure what Catherine wanted. She seemed so at home here, so comfortable, and, of course, I had the vineyard. But I didn't know if living in California full-time would be a good idea or not. All I wanted was to keep her and our baby safe and happy and to tell her all that and more…the more being kissing her again…all over her body, especially those sweet parts.

My cock twitched again, and I took a deep breath and ordered it down.

"Oh, William, look. There's my mom and dad."

It didn't take much for my arousal to fade as soon as Catherine pointed out her parents. I'd never met them, and I'd been apprehensive about it from the moment Catherine mentioned they'd be at the wedding.

Catherine had barely signaled to them when the fiftyish woman launched herself into Catherine. They had the same thick reddish brown hair and similar green eyes. A dark-haired man stood behind the woman, and I thought he must be Catherine's father, but I knew they were divorced so didn't assume.

"Daddy!" Catherine wrestled out of her mother's hold and hugged the man.

I stepped closer and smiled just as Catherine's mother gave me the once-over. I was slightly taken aback, but I kept my smile in place. Catherine had mentioned her mother was something of a cougar.

"Catherine, yum! He's even more handsome in person than in the pictures you sent."

Catherine rolled her eyes. "Mom, this is William. William, this is my mother, Jill Kelly. And this is my father, Dr. Michael Kelly."

I nodded to Jill and held out my hand to Catherine's father. "It's a pleasure, Dr. Kelly."

"It's Mick, please," he said as we shook. He gave me an awkward smile. His suit was a bit wrinkled and his hair disheveled. I knew he was a computer science professor, and he looked every bit the cerebral academic he was. Mick seemed relatively down-to-earth, especially when compared to the outgoing Jill, who had a hippy/arty thing going.

"Mick, then," I said. "So glad you could join us."

"I didn't see any photos of you, so I'm happy to finally be able to put a face to the voice I heard on the phone."

Catherine and her mother exchanged confused looks. Of course they had no idea what Mick and I were talking about. "I called Mick from Paris. To ask for Catherine's hand in marriage," I explained.

Jill sighed happily. "Mick didn't tell me, but that's so sweet! Your mother raised you right." She hugged me, and over her shoulder I saw Catherine's stunned expression. The shock turned to pleasure, and a smile broke out on her face, that same smile I wanted to put on her face every day.

The crowd around us began to clap, and we turned to the door where Beckett and Alec entered, smiling and holding hands.

The clapping reminded me of my hosting duties. "Jill, Mick, let me get you some drinks. It's time to celebrate the men of the hour."

THIRTEEN

Friday night
Catherine

I mopped up the remainder of the deconstructed jambalaya from my plate with a mini cheddar bacon biscuit, not wanting to waste a single drop. Dinner had been an amazing taste extravaganza and since I'd been ravenous, I'd enjoyed all of it. The jambalaya was my favorite, though.

Hutch and Thomas had outdone themselves with a Southern-themed feast inspired by Hutch's current Sticky Fingers menu at Morrison Hotel. "Foods of my youth," Hutch called them, but no one cooked contemporary Southern cuisine the way Hutch did. With Kellan Thomas riffing on Hutch's themes and Alejandro Vargas backing them up in the kitchen, let's just say I was glad my stomach was cooperating tonight. Kellan's Oysters Rockefeller had been *to die for*, so Alejandro's oyster adventure to Pointe Reyes this morning had definitely been worth the trouble.

Now that I was done eating, it was time to get back to work. Beckett was sitting nearby, his arm draped over Alec's shoulder. Both of them had been wearing the biggest smiles all night. And why not? They looked handsome and hip in button-down shirts and vests. And totally in love.

I grabbed my camera and made my way over to Beckett's

94

side of the table. The happy couple was busy chatting, and I was able to get some candid shoots. I took a few more of the guests, then lowered the camera and scanned the room to make sure I hadn't missed anything. Casa di Rosabela looked fabulous, inside and out. The rehearsal dinner décor was casual yet elegant, and I knew it was exactly the kind of vibe Beckett had imagined. William hadn't spared any expense, I'm sure, and the best party planners in Northern California had created a perfect setting for Beckett and Alec's celebration.

I grabbed another shot of the scene in front of me, then scrolled through the album on the camera. I still had plenty of memory, but the whole evening was there—the gorgeous meal, the chefs working in the kitchen and at the grill, the guests chatting and visiting. I smiled at a few snaps of William getting his hands dirty rolling lobster and cornbread hush puppies. It was great to see William and Hutch working side by side again tonight. William would never admit it, but I knew he was warming to Hutch. And the look on his face when he cooked with Thomas and Hutch told me he got a rush out of it.

I paged through more pictures, pausing on one of my parents. It had been kind of surreal to have William finally meet them—and vice versa—but he had completely won them over, of course. I looked back at the photo. I hadn't really noticed what was going on when I'd snapped it, but my mom was leaning into my father. It looked like he was whispering into her ear, and she was smiling at whatever he was saying, flirting even.

Very bizarre. My parents had been divorced for years, and while they were always civil to each other, they'd never acted particularly friendly. Was I crazy to think there was something going on there?

I scrolled through a few more pictures of them. I was definitely not crazy. All the body language was there. *What the fuck?* They'd been teasing and toying with each other all evening and the evidence was glaring right back at me on my own camera.

"What a beautiful evening." I turned to find my mother next to me and I quickly turned my camera off. She squeezed my shoulder.

I gave her a smile. "It really is. I'm so glad you could be here."

"We're glad we could make it, too."

We. I paused and then decided to just go for it. "So you came with Dad. Why is that?"

"Oh, honey." My mom waved her hand. "We just rode up together. It's no big deal." Then she glanced across the room at my father and smiled.

I knew that smile, and I knew my mother was deflecting the question. It wasn't *no big deal.*

"William, by the way, is wonderful. When are we going to start planning your big day? You haven't replied to my last three emails."

"Mom," I groaned. She was right, of course. She'd emailed me links to pictures of wedding dresses and to a few different venues in Santa Cruz and I'd ignored all of them. I knew she was dying to go all "mother of the bride" on me since she missed her chance the first time. It had just been me and Jace—and his brother, Jeremy, plus a few friends—at our simple courthouse wedding. We'd both told our parents after the deed with done.

I put on a big smile. "How about we just be happy for Beckett this weekend? I promise, we can talk wedding dresses and reception sites to your heart's content. But not until after all this is over, okay? One wedding at a time. Plus, Beckett needs me."

"Of course he does, honey." My mom leaned in, kissed me on the cheek, and gave me a quick hug. She knew when my mind was made up and this was her way of telling me she'd abide by my request. Until she hit me with her next question.

"Are you feeling well? I noticed you weren't drinking." Her gaze dropped to my abdomen.

Oh, fuck. Leave it to intuitive Jill Kelly to hit the nail right on the head. I knew exactly what my mom was thinking, but she was the last person I wanted to confide in *right now*. If I did, she would flip out and I was certain, before the end of the night, every single guest here would know that I was pregnant and that she was going to be a grandmother. I couldn't do that to William or to Beckett and Alec. Not tonight.

It was time to turn up my own deflection tactics. "Speaking of drinking, it looks like you're out of champagne, and there will be a toast soon. I'll go grab some more." I took her flute and handed her my camera. "Here. Take some pictures." And then I practically ran to the kitchen.

The kitchen was still a hub of activity with some staff cleaning up and others readying dessert. I paused for a moment, trying to remember why I'd come in, then remembered the champagne and headed for the wine fridge. Like everything else William owned, the wine cooler was amazing. It was custom-built and could hold over two hundred bottles of wine, storing the reds and whites at different temperatures. I'd just pulled three bottles of champagne out when I heard something *thunk* in the large walk-in pantry. I set two bottles down and opened the door.

I almost dropped the third bottle.

Holy fuck.

Zoe's leg was wrapped around Hutch's hip, and his hands were planted firmly on her ass. I did a double take. Yup, it was definitely them. They must have sensed my presence because they broke apart and stared at me.

I tried to think of something to say, but my tongue felt like it was covered in glue. Zoe eased down off Hutch, looking guilty as hell, but Hutch just raised a brow. "Need something, darlin'? Crackers? Cereal?"

I closed the door and gathered the champagne with shaking hands. My heart raced all the way back to the party. What the fuck was Hutch thinking? What about his 800-plus day celibacy streak? Surely *Zoe* wasn't worth breaking whatever self-imposed ritual he had going on.

I wanted to tell someone—no, not someone, *William*—but I couldn't just walk over and drop this bombshell on him. Not without people asking questions. Plus, I didn't even see him at the moment.

My mom had found a seat at a table and she waved at me. I veered in her direction. "Here." I handed her all three bottles of champagne and took the camera back.

"Thanks." She furrowed her brow and set the bottles on the table. "I thought you would just fill my glass."

"I—"

Hutch sauntered over and pulled out the chair across from my mom. "Why, hello, Mrs. Kelly. You must be mighty thirsty."

He indicated the bottles then gave me a dazzling smile. I'd seen that look before, and I liked to think of it as his shit-eating, kid-caught-with-his-hand-in-the-cookie jar grin. Far from looking embarrassed or apologetic, he looked entirely too pleased with himself.

I stared at him, hard, hoping he'd acknowledge me, but he wasn't having any of it. "Mom, you remember Hutch," I said, at a loss for anything else to add.

"Of course."

The two exchanged a few words, and then Hutch leaned over and whispered, "Now don't you worry, Kitty Cat. My virtue is still intact."

I rolled my eyes, but I couldn't stop a smile. Hutch was one of those people I couldn't stay mad at. Zoe, however, did not fall into the same category, and I was pissed as hell at her. She was trouble, I knew it, and the last thing Hutch needed was someone like her trampling his heart.

FOURTEEN

With Hutch occupied charming my mother, I took the opportunity to slip away to hit the ladies room and then grab a drink. My hands were still shaking and I needed to calm down. Since a shot or two of vodka was out of the question, a glass of water would have to suffice.

But when I rounded the corner on route to the powder room, I ran smack-dab into Zoe. As soon as she saw me, her expression turned stony and she sighed dramatically. I was obviously the last person she wanted to see. "What do you want?" she asked.

The hallway we were in was quiet and empty as the moment. "I don't want anything, Zoe."

"Whatever, Catherine. I'm sure you're here to lecture me. Are you going to tell me to leave your precious Hutch alone?"

I wasn't, but her tone, so confident and bitchy, made me reconsider. "He's not *my* Hutch, but we're friends. And you know what? You *should* stay away from him."

"Why? Because he deserves someone better?"

I hesitated. I hadn't expected Zoe to be so insecure. "No, because he's a really good guy, and he's gone through some pretty heavy stuff. Just stay away from him."

I wouldn't betray Hutch's confidence about his marathon sex-free streak, but I cared for him too much to let him throw everything away for Zoe, of all people.

"Cat, you're acting like his jealous ex or something."

I opened my mouth to argue but no words came out. I resented the hell out of that comment. I was not jealous. Couldn't I care about my friend without there being anything sexual about it?

Zoe filled the silence between us. "There's more to Hutch and me than you know, so why don't you just butt out?"

More to them? Had this been going on awhile? What the hell was she talking about?

"Plus," Zoe went on, "you don't have the right to talk. Maybe you should stop worrying so much about Hutch. He's a grown man who doesn't need a babysitter. If I were you, I'd be worrying about William. Remember him? Your 'fiancé'?" She used her fingers to make quote signs. "You're hurting him, you know. And it's killing me to watch you do it."

I couldn't keep quiet another second. "What are you talking about?" My cheeks burned with heat, and my eyes stung with angry tears I refused to shed. Zoe was making absolutely no sense. I wasn't hurting William.

Zoe gave an exaggerated sigh. "I know about the baby, Catherine."

I took a startled step back, feeling as though I'd been punched in the stomach—or the heart.

"I know he asked you to marry him, and even though you're wearing that ring"—it felt like a ton of bricks on my hand—"you won't set a date. You keep putting him off. He told me everything."

"I can see that," I said through clenched teeth. Now I was really seething, and my anger wasn't directed solely at Zoe.

"All he wants is to start his family with you, and you're denying him. Don't you know how much he wants this? He lost everything, and he's terrified he's going to lose you and your little bundle of joy there." She pointed at my belly, and I had the urge to cover it, protect it from the venom in her voice.

"It's killing him, Cat. *You're* killing him."

"Shut up!" I yelled, unable to leash my fury. "You don't know shit, Zoe."

"Oh, that's rich." She gave a fake laugh. "You can dish it out but you can't take it. Hey, Cat, next time you want to stick your nose into my life and tell *me* to stop playing games with Hutch, turn the mirror on yourself first."

"I am not playing games with William."

"Please. You're the Monopoly queen."

"You are such a bitch!"

At that moment, Alec's head poked around the corner. At my words, he raised his hands. "Sorry. I'll come back later."

There was still a party going on, and I had hostess duties. "Alec, no. What's up?"

"We're ready to cut the groom's cake. We can hold off."

I forced a smile. "No way. Let's go."

Zoe nodded and smiled, and I felt like smacking the smile off her face. But the person I really wanted to smack was William.

I swiped at the unshed tears making my vision blurry. I could not believe William had told Zoe I was pregnant. We promised each other not to tell anyone, not yet, and for William to confide…in *Zoe*. It felt like such a betrayal. And I was denying him? He was the one who had been denying me since Paris.

I followed Zoe back toward the terrace. I'd have to leash my anger for now. This was Beckett's night, and he deserved a wonderful cake-cutting.

Behind me, I heard Alec mutter, "Maybe we should be cutting the tension in here instead."

*****

Out on the terrace, Alec and Beckett stood at a table that held a huge sheet cake. The cake was my idea. It had a super cheesy black and white photobooth picture of the two of them printed on it with red hearts around their heads. I had it made for them, and when Beckett saw it earlier tonight, he called it the most hideous ruin of a cake he'd ever seen.

It was perfect.

Alec and Beckett held the knife together and made the first cut. Everyone clapped, and the grooms kissed and smiled into each other's eyes. It was a really romantic moment, ruined when William appeared at my side. He slid his arm around my waist, but I shifted away.

"Do not touch me!" I hissed.

He took a stunned step back.

"And don't pretend you don't know why I'm pissed. You betrayed me."

I should have known William wouldn't let it go at that. He grabbed my hand and led me away from the party, as Beckett and Alec started handing out pieces of cake. The pool house wasn't far, and he dragged me inside.

William didn't turn on the lights, probably to keep others from wandering over, so all the furnishings looked like black, menacing shapes. But I could see his face from the light filtering in from outside. Lines of concern etched between his brows. "What are you talking about, Catherine? Are you okay?"

"Am I okay?" I barely managed to leash my fury. "No, I am *not* okay. You told Zoe. How could you!"

His eyed flicked down and away from my face, which was confirmation of what I already knew. It pissed me off all over again.

"I haven't even told my mom, William. My own *mother*! She's acting like she suspects something, but I promised you, and I kept my promise. But you—you! Zoe, William? Why her? She hates me and now she has her claws in Hutch. I caught the two of them making out in your pantry."

"What?" His brows arched up in surprise. Obviously, he didn't know about Hutch and Zoe. "Catherine." He tried to take my hand, but I snatched it back. His mouth settled in that firm line that indicated he was annoyed and confused. "What are you mad about— Zoe and Hutch or Zoe knowing that you're pregnant?"

"You just don't get it, do you?" I said, throwing my arms up. "You aren't even sorry you betrayed me."

"Betrayed you? I didn't betray you. I confided in my cousin.

I have to have someone to talk to, since you aren't talking to me."

The words stung, just as I was sure he intended.

"I'm not talking to you? You're the one not talking to me!" I sliced my hand through the air. William caught it.

"Bullshit, Catherine, and you know it. Every time I try to bring up anything important, about marrying you, about the baby, our future, you stiffen up and avoid the topic. Are you or aren't you going to marry me?"

"I am!"

"Fine. When?" He released my hand and crossed his arms over his chest.

"I don't know yet." I wanted to put the argument back on him. "Why are you pushing this?"

"Because I want you to be my wife. I want to start my life with you and something is holding you back. But hell if I know what it is because you won't tell me." He was almost yelling, and my head had begun to pound.

I couldn't do this right now. William was right and he was wrong, and it didn't change that I was pissed as hell that he'd betrayed my trust.

"This isn't the time or the place." I turned my back and yanked open the door to the pool house. "I'm going to bed."

Surprisingly, William let me walk away.

I couldn't just leave the party without saying my good nights. I quickly made my rounds, kissing my mom and dad goodbye. They were both staying at a quaint inn in downtown St. Helena. Separate rooms, thank god.

Finally, I approached Beckett and Alec, who were enjoying their cake. "Cat, did you get a piece?" Beckett asked then got a look at my face. "What's wrong?"

"I have a headache. Sorry to bail early." I kissed his cheek and hugged Alec. "See you in the morning, okay?"

Beckett squeezed my shoulder, and I held it together until I made it inside. Then the tears slipped down my cheeks and I sprinted for the stairs and the sanctuary of the master suite.

I flopped on the bed and let the tears flow. He said *I* wasn't talking when he was the one who had been avoiding everything—sex, serious conversation—for the past month. But William was right that something was holding me back from marrying him. I wanted to be his wife, but every time I really stopped to think about it, I got scared. I'd already been married once and I'd lost everything. Taking that step again was big, maybe too big right now. I'd tried to keep William at a distance from the start because losing Jace at twenty-two had really messed me up.

William knew that. I thought he'd understood that.

And now I'd barely known William a few months and he expected me to take that monumental step again. He expected me to lay it all on the line. Again.

Then there was the baby.

Everyone would think I got pregnant to trap William into marrying me. I'd been down this road before, been vilified by my husband's friends and family, by total strangers. I didn't want

William's family and friends sighting me in their targets just like Jace's had. And it would be worse this time. William was rich and prominent already and he was going to become even wealthier once he turned 30 this fall. The timing of all of this didn't look good, that was for sure.

I thought about what Zoe had said to me. *All he wants is to start his family with you, and you're denying him. Don't you know how much he wants this? He lost everything, and he's terrified he's going to lose you and your little bundle of joy there.* I wish I could doubt her words, and it killed me to think that my indecision was truly hurting him. But maybe if William and I were talking about the baby, if I knew how he felt about the pregnancy, I wouldn't be so scared of walking down the aisle. Most of the time, I thought William was happy, but if what Zoe said was true, he wasn't. Why hadn't he'd told me that? Something was still holding *him* back. Something had kept him from making love to me for the past month.

A part of me, a really big part, wanted to be all in. I *needed* to be all in, but the fear made a knot in my stomach that I couldn't push away.

Wiping my tears, I pulled on a T-shirt and a pair of red lacy boy shorts, scrubbed my face in the bathroom, and climbed into the big bed. The sounds of the party had died down, but William hadn't come up yet.

Silent tears ran down my face until I fell asleep.

Alone.

FIFTEEN

Friday night
William

I couldn't remember the last time I'd had a night out with the guys. Cigars, bourbon, a fire—it was exactly what I needed at the moment. Usually I took my frustrations out on the treadmill. I took the same approach to my health as I do to my business: I am exact and strict in everything I do. I had no doubt that a long hard run would have done wonders to ease the tension I was feeling following my fight with Catherine. But as I surveyed the circle of men hanging out by the outdoor fire pit, I decided that bourbon would be even better.

Beckett and Alec sat beside Morrison, who'd taken the chair next to me. On my other side were Thomas; Beckett's brother-in-law, Aidan; Vargas, since he was staying out at the house anyway; and Dr. Kelly. I had to keep reminding myself to call him Mick. Mick was my fiancé's father, so I couldn't shake the need for formality.

The talk had started with cigars. Kellan was a cigar aficionado, and he'd pulled out several Cubans. I passed, but Morrison, Vargas, and Mick had stogies clamped between their teeth. Aidan looked at them longingly.

"Sure you don't want one?" Kellan waved the cigar at Beckett's brother-in-law.

109

"Lucia will kill me if I come to bed smelling like cigar smoke."

Morrison made a whipped sound, and Aidan held up his hands. "Hey, I'm not complaining. I love that woman. You know what they say, happy wife, happy life."

"Good answer," Beckett said, reaching over to clink his glass with Aidan's.

"I'm always being watched," Aidan joked. "Either by Lucia or by Cole. But seriously, kids make all the difference, man. Your whole life changes. In a good way."

Aidan had my attention now. I leaned forward and rested my elbows on my knees, my drink dangling between. I knew Aidan was a successful lawyer, so his work-life balance would be similar to mine. I didn't have many close male friends—my business didn't allow for them—so there was no one I could ask for advice.

"You go from barely having your shit together to having to act like a role model. You can't swear, can't smoke, can't drink—not in front of the kid anyway. Kids are crazy, man, they're always watching and listening."

"My nephew is a great kid," Beckett said. "You must be doing something right."

"That's the worst of it," Aidan admitted with a groan. "After a while you don't even really mind that you're home on Friday night watching Elmo instead of hanging at the bar with your friends."

"There'll be time for that again," Mick said. He hadn't spoken a lot tonight, but he had a quiet presence that spoke louder than a lot of the bullshit the guys were throwing around. "Blink and your little girl is all grown up and getting married." He glanced at me, and I raised my glass to him. I knew this was an emotional time for him.

When I let myself go there, which I rarely did, I found myself wishing my family could be a part of this weekend, part of my life. I knew my mother would have loved Catherine. She would have been thrilled that we were getting married. That is if tonight's fight hadn't completely changed Catherine's mind.

Catherine and I *should* be getting married. Usually it was the guy with the commitment issues, the guy who wouldn't step up. I couldn't believe Catherine had the gall to accuse me of not opening up, when it was obvious to me that she was not allowing herself to move forward with her life. Even a baby on the way wasn't enough to get her to fully commit to me. If she would only fucking talk to me about it, I could reassure her that I didn't want to take Jace's place in her life, but that I wanted to move forward together, as a family. Hell, I was scared to death of becoming a father, but I believed I could step up with Catherine by my side. But now it all seemed so fragile.

As I'd been lost in thought, the conversation had shifted to baseball, and hackles were up.

"So you're telling me this is the Cubs' year?" Vargas shook his head at Alec's argument.

"Have you seen Lester pitch?" Alec demanded. "I'm saying they have a shot."

"Aw, come on man. They're the Lovable Losers. Maddon might as well hang it up."

"Maddon never does what you expect," Morrison added, surprising me. I didn't know he was a Cubs' fan. "He's unconventional."

"He can do whatever the fuck he wants," Vargas said, sipping his tequila. "The Giants will smoke the Cubs like they do every year."

Those were fighting words, and I sat back to watch the ribbing. My head was all over the place, so I wasn't participating in the conversation much tonight.

"You talk big when it comes to the Giants, but what are the Forty-niners going to do this year?" Beckett demanded. "You lost your coach and four players." He started ticking off the players who'd retired.

I turned from the fire to look up at the house. Catherine was probably sleeping by now. I'd wanted to follow her when she'd stormed out of the pool house, but what was I going to say? Maybe space was exactly what she needed. Maybe it was what I needed, too. I was never going to get used to seeing her beautiful green eyes fill with tears. It slayed me every time, and if I was the cause of those tears, my first urge was to punch something. Hard.

I took another swallow of bourbon. It took the edge off, but my anger was still simmering.

"Hey, Lambourne, did you hear me?" Kellan must have asked me a couple of times because everyone was looking at me.

"Sorry. What'd you say?"

"I was saying how much I admired your '69 Speedster. Anyone besides Beckett and Alec allowed to take it for a spin?"

I'd told Beckett to drive it this afternoon when he and Alec took off for a few hours.

"I don't know, Kellan. I've seen that piece of shit SUV you drive. You think you can handle a vintage Porsche?"

Kellan laughed. "You know why I drive that piece of shit SUV? Because I drive it to the farmer's markets and fill it up with produce. Everything in California now is local and organic and vegan. If I want to drive a car without chia seeds in it, I take Electra's."

"It's not the vegans that kill me," Beckett said. "I can make some killer vegan cupcakes, donuts, you name it. It's all the gluten-free bullshit. I can make you a gluten-free cake, but don't expect it to rock your world."

Alec patted his shoulder. "You add all the gluten you want to our wedding cake, sweetie." Beckett leaned over and gave his soon-to-be-husband a kiss.

"Bet I can guess where your head is right now," Morrison said to me, his voice low so only I could hear. "I saw Cat storm out of the pool house. I get the feeling I'm partly to blame. I'm sure Catherine told you."

That was right. I'd forgotten Catherine had said she'd seen Hutch and Zoe together. "She did mention she caught you taking advantage of my cousin."

Hutch threw back his head and laughed. "If you think I took advantage of her, you don't know your cousin as well as you think you do."

In spite of myself, I smiled, conceding the point. I didn't want to like Morrison, but sometimes it was hard to remember that. "Maybe you're the one I need to look out for. Zoe can be a ballbuster."

"Don't I know it." He sat back and stared at the glowing end of his cigar. "Mind if I give you a piece of advice?" He looked at me. "About Catherine?"

I stiffened. I might have been at a loss for what to say to Catherine, but Morrison was the last person I wanted advice from. I restrained the urge to put him in his place. "Go ahead."

"Yeah, that tone made it sound like you don't mind at all. All I ask is that you don't punch me in the face. I want to look pretty tomorrow."

"What's the advice, Morrison?"

He held up a hand. "Some of this has been passed down from father to son. I need you to give it the respect it deserves."

I swallowed more bourbon to keep from punching him, like I promised.

"The first bit of advice comes from my Granddaddy Morrison. He told me that if you want to know what a woman will look like fifty years from now, take a gander at her mama. I think you're safe there, William."

"Easy there," Mick chimed in. He'd overheard Morrison's pronouncement.

"My apologies, sir, but you have a beautiful ex-wife, as I'm sure you'll agree."

To that Mick smiled and held up his drink in a toast across the fire.

The last thing that worried me about Catherine's mother was her appearance. I was more worried she'd grab my ass when we were alone, but I wasn't about to tell Mick or Morrison that.

"The second piece of advice came from my Daddy. He told me, 'Son, all women are crazy. You just gotta find the one that's the least crazy.'"

I chortled at the one. "Good luck with Zoe then."

Morrison ignored my jibe. "Cat is relatively low on the crazy scale, so you're two for two, Lambourne. You did good by locking that down."

I set my empty glass down and folded my arms. "Do you have any real advice?"

"Hey, I'm giving you gold here. One more, the last bit of advice. This doesn't come from my daddy but from me. You ready for this, Lambourne?"

I raised my brows as an indication for him to continue.

"Okay, here it is. *Talk to her.*"

His tone hit a nerve. *What does Morrison know?* "I have been talking to her. That's what we were doing when you saw her leave the pool house."

Morrison shook his head. "Nope. That just tells me you're not talking enough. Most women—and Catherine falls into this category—can't get enough talking." He made opening and closing motions with his hands. "They want to talk everything out, and the big stuff? You have to talk that out until you have covered every angle. Every. Angle. " He gave me a long look.

Damn it. I hated that he was on to something.

"I get the sense that right now you both have some big stuff on your plate. I know that Cat hasn't called any of the job leads our cookbook project has brought her way. I can't get her to tell me why. Maybe you know, but the more I think about it, the more I'm pretty sure there's something bigger going on."

I didn't know about the jobs. I didn't know that Catherine had gotten more offers or that she wasn't responding. It irked me that Morrison knew this about her, but more so that she hadn't told me.

Morrison watched me absorbing his words in silence, then went on, "Take it or leave it." He leaned close again. "But I suggest you take it."

I needed some more bourbon.

"So Hutch," Vargas called across the fire. "I hear you were a big rock star once upon a time."

Hutch raised his glass, falling back into the group conversation easily. "Sex, drugs, and rock and roll. It's the American way."

"You holding out on us, man? What was the band?"

"Elysium. Soul-crushing Southern rock that could break your heart and your ear drums at the same time. We were loud, man. I'm lucky I can still hear."

"I always wanted to be a rock star." Beckett mused and Alec burst out laughing.

"What?" Beckett asked.

"I love you, honey, but you sing worth shit"

We all laughed at this.

"Tell us, Hutch, what's the craziest thing that ever happened when you were a rock star? I'm talking the really freaky shit." Vargas asked. As the youngest among us, he no doubt loved the idea of a rock-n-roll lifestyle.

For a moment, Morrison's face looked tight and strained. Then it relaxed again. "The craziest shit went down in L.A. No surprise, right? It was after a show, and there were these five chicks, every single one of them smokin' hot. I'm talkin' tens, all of them..."

I glanced up at the house again as Morrison continued his story. I didn't like to admit it, but Morrison was right. I did need to talk to Catherine. I needed to know what was going on in her head. Whatever it was, we had to make it right before we could go forward.

And I wanted the date set. I wanted Catherine as my wife. She should have been Mrs. Lambourne already.

SIXTEEN

Saturday morning
Catherine

I woke alone. William's side of the bed didn't look touched, but I spotted a note on his pillow.

Smelled like bourbon and cigars. Slept in a guest casita. Didn't want to wake you. Going to the gym and then the olive grove to check on the set up. Come find me. We need to talk.

~WML

We did need to talk. My anger had cooled, and I could think more clearly by the cold light of day. It probably also helped that William had left that note—he knew I hated waking up and not knowing where he was. His tendency to disappear without even a goodbye had been the cause of one of our very first arguments. Now, he always made sure to let me know where he was.

I'd try to remember that he could be thoughtful the next time we fought.

I glanced down at my Patek Philippe. I didn't have time to find William now. I was already running late, and Beckett needed me to help him get ready. This was his big day. I needed to put all the stuff with William and Zoe aside, for now. If I started thinking about it again, I'd just get worked up and today wasn't about me. It was my best friend's wedding day, and I had to be there for him.

I threw on some Lululemon yoga pants and a flowy tank, threw my hair in a ponytail, and rushed to the guest quarters where Beckett would be getting ready. I detoured through the kitchen to grab a bottle of water and almost knocked over the photography student I'd hired.

"Sidney!" I grabbed her shoulder to steady her. "I am so sorry."

"That's okay." Sidney smiled and held out her hands as though to say *no harm done.* She had mocha skin, curly black hair, and the most expressive brown eyes. She had a great eye behind the camera, too, and she was an excellent photographer. Since Alec and Beckett were getting ready in different rooms and I wanted pictures of both of them plus Beckett and me, I'd hired Sidney. No way I could be everywhere, and I needed to be with Beckett if nerves took over.

"Actually, I'm glad we ran into each other—no pun intended. Let me give you the itinerary." I filled her in on the day's events and where I needed her, then I grabbed my camera bag and had her follow me outside to the row of guest casitas. "This is where Alec is getting ready with his sister and his best friend. And two down is where Beckett and I will be."

She made a note on a pad. "Cool. I'll start with Alec, if that's okay."

"That's great."

I left her knocking on Alec's door and headed to Beckett's casita.

I knocked and opened the door. "Where's the groom?" I sang.

"In the bedroom!"

I stepped into the one-bedroom suite. Like everything else at Casa di Rosabela, the casitas were spacious and luxurious. The door opened into parlor with double sliding glass doors showcasing a view of the vineyard and mountains. On one side was a dining table and a small kitchen, and on the other, a sitting area with a mounted big screen TV and a travertine fireplace. The décor was California contemporary with a mission flare, generally neutral with pops of color. The bedroom was through a door off the dining area. I knew it had a king-size bed and a gorgeous bathroom with a sunken marble tub and a separate shower area.

I headed for the bedroom, and when I reached the door, Beckett tugged me inside. "Cat!"

I could see from his watery eyes tears were imminent.

"I'm so glad you're here."

"I was giving the photography assistant I hired the rundown. What's wrong?"

A quick rap sounded on the outer door. "I have breakfast!"

I glanced out the bedroom door and saw Fernanda with a tray balanced on her arm. "I have coffee, pastries from Mr. Hutch, and fruit." She bustled in. "Where would you like me to put it?"

"In here, Fernanda." When she came into the bedroom, I indicated a glass table in the corner of the room by a window.

"Oh, Mr. Beckett," Fernanda gushed, setting eyes on my best friend. "So handsome. So happy." She came over and gave him a hug. They had been spending so much time in the kitchen together, no doubt they'd grown close.

When Fernanda left, Beckett retreated to a chair in front of a vanity with a long counter and soft lighting. White and pink lilies sat in a vase before him. "Beckett, what's wrong?"

"Nothing." He waved a hand. "It's just I can't believe today is the day." He fanned himself. "I'm trying so hard not to cry. I'm so happy."

I could feel my tears welling up, too. Beckett was crying tears of joy, not sadness. Seeing him so happy made me extra emotional. I hugged him hard, resting my head on his shoulder.

"You and Alec are going to be so happy together. You're going to remember this day for the rest of your life."

Just like I'd always remember my wedding to Jace. I'd been emotional that day, so happy and scared and eager for a new chapter in my life. I couldn't help but think about my wedding to William— assuming he did still want to marry me. I could see myself in the white dress, walking down the aisle to meet my gorgeous groom.

Just picturing it made my stomach knot. My wedding to Jace, for what it was, had been picture-perfect, too, and the lovely picture had crumpled. I knew that I needed to stop comparing the two, but it was easier said than done.

Pictures! I had better get to work.

I squeezed Beckett in another embrace. "I'm so thrilled for you, B."

I pulled my camera out of my bag and snapped a picture of the room. I wanted to capture all the pre-wedding details: his suit laid out on the bed, the tray of breakfast food, and Beckett in front of the mirror. "You and Alec are perfect for each other."

"So are you and William," Beckett said, catching my eye in the mirror when I set my camera down.

I put my hands on my hips, looking around for something to do—anything but start this conversation. "Let's not talk about me today. Want some coffee or a plate with one of Hutch's pastries? They look delicious."

He grabbed my hand before I could rush for the tray. "What I want is for you to listen." I turned and looked down at him. His voice was so serious, and his blue eyes so earnest. "I can see what you're doing, Cat."

"Documenting your big day?" I said, trying one last time to avoid the topic.

"No, Miss Hamlet. You're overthinking your relationship with William, as usual I knew something was up last night at the fire pit, but I can't read William like I can you."

So William had looked upset last night? I wasn't the only one then.

"There's nothing to read, Beckett. This is your day. No 'Cat and William drama' allowed."

"You're right." He stood and pushed away from the mirror.

"It is my day, and since I'm your best friend and I've always given it to you straight and it is—as you said—my wedding day, I get to do and say exactly what I want."

I sighed and sank into a plush armchair. I wasn't going to get out of this.

"You, Cat, deserve to be happy," Beckett announced. "You deserve everything that has come your way. And I can see you second-guessing all of it. I can see you looking for the cracks."

I tried to bite back tears. I knew what he was going to say and I loved that he felt comfortable enough to say it to my face—no matter how much I didn't want to hear it. "Beckett—"

Beckett raised a finger. "I'm talking here. Here's my advice: live for now. Your past doesn't define you, and it exists only in your mind if you let it. Stop dwelling. Stop wasting time on it. Your future is full of possibilities and hasn't even happened yet. Don't worry about it."

My eyes burned with unshed tears, and Beckett knelt before the chair and took my hand. I had to choke back a sob.

"This moment. That's all you have. And what do you have? A loving family, great friends, a man who absolutely adores you. He really loves you, Cat. It's written all over him and everyone can see it. He's a good guy and I know you two have been through some shit together, but he won't hurt you."

I swiped at the tears threatening to spill and shook my head. "I know, Beckett. I know."

"And—Cat!—a baby," Beckett said softly. "You're having a

baby together. You're going to be a mom. I know you didn't plan it, but come on. It was clearly meant to be. Could you have imagined a better life for yourself?"

My hands instinctively went to my abdomen and I felt the tight curve of my mini bump. I *couldn't* have imagined a better life. Beckett was right, as usual. I had everything I'd ever wanted—more, even—and I'd be a fool to let it slip through my fingers. And I'd be an even bigger fool to throw it away because I was so afraid of losing it. "You know something, Beckett?" I said with a sniff.

"I'm right?"

I gave him a playful shove. "Yes, but I was going to say that you make an amazing bride. I'm the one who's supposed to give you advice, but here you are being all wise and thoughtful."

"That's me. Wise and thoughtful."

"Come here, you." I hugged him hard, so thankful to have a best friend like Beckett. We pulled back and smiled at each other, and I heard a click.

"That was perfect," Sid said. "Sorry. I hope it's okay that I snuck in to get a few candid shots of you two getting ready."

"It's totally okay," I told her. "I'm glad you got that one. But now"—I snatched a Kleenex and dabbed at my red nose—"I'm going to grab a shower and hope the hot water gets rid of all this red splotchy skin."

"Bathroom is all yours," Beckett said. "Your dress is hanging on the door."

The plan had been for us to get ready together, so I'd already stashed a toiletry bag in his bathroom. I showered and shaved my legs then toweled off and dried my hair. I could have brought in a stylist to do my hair and makeup, but I didn't want all the fuss. I fluffed and piled my hair into a messy bun, leaving some tresses down for a wispy effect. I used light makeup with some bronzer to create a glowy look.

Finally, I slipped into my dress. It was a vintage pale blue silk chiffon long slip dress with beautiful embroidery along the edges and delicate, thin straps. Beckett and Alec were wearing matching light grey suits with waistcoats and blue ties that were just a few shades darker than my dress.

By the time I slipped my strappy sandals on and stepped back into the bedroom, Beckett had dressed in his suit and was fumbling with his cufflinks.

"Cat, you look amazing. Like a goddess." He beamed when I stepped out. I twirled for him.

"You look amazing, too. We're just like Julia Roberts and Dermott Mulroney in *My Best Friend's Wedding* because we're really best friends and this is your wedding. Which I guess makes Alec Cameron Diaz." I snorted with laughter.

Beckett groaned and rolled his eyes. "Oh my God, you are so lame. Please stop. And seriously, you need to get over your Julia Roberts obsession. It's unhealthy."

"Fine," I said, but I was still laughing. "Here, let me help you with those." Sid had come back and was snapping away as I threaded the cufflink through the opening in Beckett's sleeve.

Once both cufflinks were in place, Beckett shook out his arms and struck a pose. "What do you think?"

"I think you look hot. Seriously, Alec is going to flip when he sees you. Hold on." I grabbed my phone and held it up for a selfie. It wasn't professional, by any means, but this was best friends on a wedding day—perfect Insta-fodder.

Then I reached into my clutch and pulled out the envelope I'd been saving for this moment. "Before we go get you married, I have something for you."

Beckett took it, his eyes narrowed with suspicion and a small smile playing on his lips. He shook it. "A pony, right? I've always wanted a pony."

"Not a pony. Something better."

"Better than a pony? We'll see." He ripped the envelope open and furrowed his brow at the key that fell into his hand. Tied around it was Jace's shark tooth necklace. I'd found the necklace in a box when I was moving all of my things to William's Chicago penthouse.

"That was Jace's good luck charm and he never took it off," I said, indicating the necklace. "Now it's yours."

Jace had been Beckett's friend, too, so I knew the necklace would mean a lot to him. "And the key?" Beckett asked, his voice trembling.

"That's the key to my condo. Well, to your condo. I'm giving it to you."

He shook his head. "Cat, are you nuts?" He tried to push the key back into my hand, but I put my hands behind my back. "You can't just give me your condo. I cannot accept this."

I held up my hand. "Beckett, I know how much you love it and the AGA and the kitchen. It's wasted on me, and the truth is, I don't live there anymore. So I'd really like for you and Alec to have it."

"No fucking way. It's worth a ton of money. I know what you paid for it. You are certifiably nuts. I can't possibly…"

I cut him off. "Yes, you can. And it's already yours. All the paperwork is done and I transferred the title to you. Do whatever you want with it—live in it, rent it out, sell it. You helped me find it and you saved me, Beckett. After Jace died…" My voice trailed off as I took a big gulping breath and vowed not to cry. This was a happy moment, and Beckett deserved this. I smiled up at him. "You gave me a new start right when I needed it the most. I can't ever really repay you for that, Beckett. Ever. But I can give you a fabulous wedding present, can't I?"

"Cat…" He blew out a breath, and I knew I was winning.

"Come on. I know you love that AGA, and now you can put it to good use, cooking for your new husband. I really, really want you guys to have it. Please, I want to do this. Say yes."

He stared at me a long time, his eyes watering. "Yes." Beckett pulled me into another hug. "And stop doing nice things now or I'll cry and look all red at my own wedding."

"Got it. Nothing else nice." I had to wipe away the tears threatening to spill from my own eyes before they smeared my mascara.

"Thank you, Cat," Beckett whispered into my hair. "I'm only saying yes because I know you can afford it, future Mrs. Lambourne." He squeezed me and pulled back, smiling.

"Yes, I can." I had to admit, it felt good to say that.

As usual, Beckett understood perfectly. The key was more than a gift. It was the last vestige of Catherine Kelly. I suddenly realized what I'd known for a long time. William was my home now, no matter where we were.

I glanced down at my watch and took a deep breath. "Looks like it's time to get this show on the road. You ready?"

Beckett nodded, placing the key on the vanity. "Ready."

Hands clasped together, we headed out.

SEVENTEEN

We couldn't have asked for a better day to host an outdoor wedding. William had probably called in a favor from the weather gods to make it happen. It was just before 11 in the morning, and the sun was almost overhead, which meant everything was perfectly lit. The sky was a bright cerulean, not a cloud marring the vast stretch of blue. The temperature was warm, but not hot, and a light breeze ruffled my dress.

Beckett and I had worked out the wedding set-up, but neither of us had had time to implement it. William had been in charge of making sure it happened like Beckett imagined, and he'd gone above and beyond. The officiant stood at a white pergola that was perched at the edge of the olive grove. It was overrun with wildly curling vines in deep green. Behind it, the vineyard stretched into the horizon as far as we could see. It made a breathtaking backdrop of green, gold, and brown with the hills in the distance shimmery with sunlight.

White chairs had been set on either side of the pergola, and a white runner rippled down the resulting aisle. Pink peonies were tied at the start of each aisle, providing a splash of color. Off to the left of the pergola, a string quartet was seated and ready.

I was glad I had a job to do. I was excited and nervous for Beckett, and it helped to keep busy. Since nature had provided the perfect lighting, Sid and I snapped away at the set-up, the landscape, and then the arriving guests. We worked well together, and she seemed to know when I rathered she take the shots that would have been more too difficult for me to manage in heels and a long dress.

Finally, the chairs were almost full. I bit my lip when I scanned the guests and didn't see Beckett's parents. I'd really hoped they'd change their minds and come. He'd said Lucia, Aidan, and Cole being here was enough, but it would have meant so much to him if his mom and dad had come, too. Maybe one day they'd be ready to accept their son's marriage to another man. At least Beckett was happy and had finally found someone to spend his life with.

The string quartet launched into an instrumental rendition of "I Choose You," by Sara Bareilles, and I knew that was my cue. I stowed my camera in its bag and tucked it under the table holding programs and a book for guests to sign. My bouquet was also on the table, and I took a deep breath and lifted the flowers by their ribbon-wrapped stems. The peonies all but exploded in various colors of pink.

"Is it straight?" Caleb, Alec's best friend, asked and pointed to the peony pinned to his lapel.

I gave him the thumbs up. "You ready for this?"

"I'm ready for the reception afterward. See you on the other side."

I clutched the flowers tightly, pasted on a smile, and walked slowly down the aisle. About a quarter of the way, my fake smile turned genuine as I spotted my parents, Aidan and little Cole, plus a few more mutual friends of Beckett's and mine from Chicago, then Hutch. It was perfect.

Caleb followed me down the aisle then stopped opposite me at the pergola. The officiant, a woman in her mid-fifties with brown hair she'd braided so it flowed down her back in a long tail, smiled at us. She handed me the second camera I'd asked be available, and I whispered my thanks.

The string quartet paused, then played again, the music crescendoing. Beckett started down the aisle with his sister Lucia on his arm. I snapped pictures of the pair, wanting to catch Lucia's elated expression. Beckett looked so handsome, and I'd never seen his smile so huge. Tears blurred my eyes for the next few shots, but I managed to blink them out of the way and snap a shot of Lucia hugging Beckett at the pergola before taking her seat next to her husband and son.

Without looking at me, Beckett reached out and clasped my hand. I squeezed it, and we both drew in excited breaths as Alec appeared. His mother was on one side and his father on the other. They looked at their son with adoration, and why wouldn't they? Alec looked gorgeous in his grey suit and waistcoat. I snapped a few pictures of Alec, but left most of those shots to Sid. As Alec's parents kissed his cheeks and embraced him, I stowed the camera again and stepped back beside Beckett .Alec's parents took their seats in the front row, and Alec and Beckett turned to each other and then toward the officiant.

She began the service with a few words about each of them, her impressions when she'd met them, and how perfect they were for each other. Now that I didn't have the camera in my hand and Beckett was gazing lovingly at Alec, I was able to scan the guests. I'd known where William was all along, but I hadn't wanted to look at him because I was afraid he'd distract me from my maid of honor duties.

Now my gaze met his. He sat in the front row, diagonal to me. As usual, looking at him took my breath away. He was so incredibly handsome with his thick dark hair curling just at his collar. I'd forgotten to nag him about getting a haircut. Or maybe I hadn't wanted to because I liked his non-corporate look so much. His eyes were almost as blue as the sky, and the planes of his face looked like they'd been chiseled by a sculptor. He wore one of my favorite suits, a charcoal grey Tom Ford with a pink tie that matched my bouquet.

The look of longing he gave me was so intense my heart ached. How had I failed to see it before? How had I failed to see how much he wanted me to be his wife? Anyone looking at his face right now could have seen how much he wanted it to be us standing up there.

I had been such a fool to argue with him last night. I needed to make this right between us. I looked at Beckett and Alec, so happy they beamed at each other. That should be William and me.

That *would* be William and me.

Alec and Beckett had written their own vows, and even though I'd heard them before, I listened again because they were funny and sweet at the same time. Alec promised to eat all of Beckett's culinary creations, even the ones with cranberries though he hated cranberries, and Beckett promised to eat at Alec's favorite fast food joint, the Wiener Circle, at least once a quarter.

Compromise—that was what marriage was all about. It was about staying true to yourself while becoming part of something so much more than you alone. I was good alone, but I knew I was better with William. We'd made it through the petty relationship fights every couple had, but we'd also managed to survive through some really big stuff, too. We'd broken up and gotten back together again because no matter what hit us, we belonged together.

Finally, the officiant told Beckett and Alec they could kiss, and the guests erupted into applause and cheers. I hugged both of them before following them back down the aisle.

*****

The dining room and terrace were filled with tables, and servers were ready to circle with appetizers and champagne.

I made it inside after the wedding party pictures were done, just as lunch was about to be served, and took a seat with William at a table with my parents. He pulled my chair out when I sat, and whispered, "You look beautiful."

I clutched his hand and met his eyes, silently letting him know we would talk later. "Thank you."

William sat down beside me, and the servers brought the first course: a tiny lobster spring roll set in a lemongrass consommé. I knew the menu for today was filled with highly refined classic French cuisine—the kind Beckett loved and the kind Hutch excelled at making. But the addition of Kellan Thomas to the kitchen meant Beckett and Alec's wedding luncheon had gone from an exceptional meal to a truly extraordinary culinary event.

I'd been a little leery of sitting with my parents. I'd endured more than one uncomfortable dinner with the two of them, but apparently their congeniality at the rehearsal dinner was not a fluke. They were still getting along.

"The wedding was beautiful, just beautiful," my mom said as we dug into our spring rolls.

"It reminded me a little of our wedding," my dad replied.

"Did it?" My mother turned to him and put a hand on his arm. "How so?"

"Both outdoors on perfect sunny days in the spring. Both full of happy people." He grinned at my mom. "My bride was more beautiful, of course."

My mother giggled.

What the hell was going on here?

I exchanged a 'what-the-fuck look' with William, but he just shrugged as if to say, 'Let them be happy.'

The rest of lunch felt like a blur. The food was incredible, of course. The lobster spring roll was followed by a baby white asparagus soup with a polenta beignet, mushrooms, and fresh herbs.

I smiled at that one, recognizing Hutch's Southern influence on the dish. Next came a delicate piece of sautéed Pacific striped bass with saffron and lemon garnished with tiny little clams William said were called coquinas. It was a meal of many courses and small portions, all of which looked like art on the plate.

By the sixth or seventh course—I'd lost count—I was pleasantly full but determined to finish the delicious lamb in a rich wine sauce served over Gruyere grits with Brussel sprouts and roasted turnips. It was too good *not* to eat.

William was in epicurean heaven, I could tell. This was an once-in-a-lifetime meal and he seemed to be enjoying every bite of it, not to mention the artistry and skill that went into each and every dish. Kellan Thomas and Hutch Morrison together really were unbeatable.

But even the fabulous food couldn't alleviate the obvious tension at our table. My parents were getting along, so it wasn't because of them. It was me and William. There was so much that we both needed to say that we were being awkward with one another. We were avoiding eye contact and being very polite in our exchanges. Even my mother gave me a concerned look.

Finally, once the meal was finished and all of the family dances were over, the rest of the guests began to join Alec and Beckett on the dance floor. William held out a hand to me. "May I have this dance?"

I smiled up at him. "I'd like that."

The band was playing "I Only Have Eyes for You," and William led me to the center of the dance floor. I moved into his arms effortlessly, sighing with pleasure when he pulled me close.

"I missed you last night," he whispered in my ear. I shivered at the feel of his warm breath on my neck.

"I missed you, too. I'm sorry we argued."

"Me, too." He pulled me close, his hand on my back sliding down to my waist and barely skimming the curve of my ass. Instantly my heart fluttered with excitement and a low burn began in my belly. It was always like this with William. Whenever he touched me or held me, my body responded to him. I wished we were alone, so I could kiss him, stroke him, feel his bare skin on mine.

I laid my cheek on his shoulder, inhaling his scent. His hard body moved slowly against mine. I felt safe in his arms. This was where I was meant to be, where I belonged. This was home.

And then suddenly I realized what I needed to do.

EIGHTEEN

I hadn't planned to go on Beckett and Alec's honeymoon with them, but when they waved goodbye to the guests and hopped in the back of the big black SUV Asa was driving, I got in after them.

"I'll be back later and Asa will be with me, so don't worry. There's just something I need to do." I gave William an apologetic smile as we closed the door and Asa started the car. William had looked surprised, too stunned to argue or try to stop me.

"Um, Cat." Beckett stared at me. "What are you doing?"

"Going with you to the airport." I settled back in the seat and turned to face the newlyweds. "I won't get on William's plane with you, I promise. Tropos is all yours for the next 10 days."

"Heaven!" Alec leaned back and sighed.

Beckett wasn't mollified. "And what about all the guests? You just left them. And William?"

"William can handle them. And he'll be fine. Just trust me, okay?"

He crossed his arms over his chest and tapped his fingers, waiting.

"All right. There's just something I need to do after we drop you at the airport. I knew if I didn't go now, I'd never get away. So, sorry to crash your party, but go ahead. Open the champagne and do kissy newlywed things. Pretend I'm not even here."

Beckett lifted the champagne bottle and handed it to Alec. "You do this one. I've opened more than enough champagne bottles in the last few months," he said, referring to our champagne pop shoot for WML Champagne. He pointed a finger at me. "And you, Miss Dark and Mysterious. When we get back from Tropos, I want to know what this was all about. Promise?"

"Promise."

The trip to the airport was pretty fun after that. Beckett and Alec drank champagne, I drank bottled water, and we talked about the wedding and the toasts and all the incredible food. Alec and I both praised Beckett's wedding cake. It had been just as delicious as Hutch and Kellan's many courses, more so maybe because it had been chocolate.

The drive was pretty quick for an early Saturday afternoon and we arrived at Napa County Airport in less than an hour. When Asa dropped the guys at the private terminal where one of William's jets awaited to fly them to the Caribbean, I gave them both hugs. I was genuinely teary-eyed. I'd miss them, even if I'd see them again in a couple of weeks.

When the door closed, Asa looked back at me. "Want to tell me what's up, Miss Cat?"

"I need a favor from you, Asa."

"I had a feeling you were going to say that."

I held up a hand. "It's not a secret. You can call William and tell him if you want. But I need you to drive me to the beach. In Santa Cruz."

Asa hesitated before answering me. "That's over a hundred miles away."

"I know. We probably won't get back to St. Helena until tonight, but I really need to go. Now. I'll tell you the way to the beach I want when we get close."

He took a long breath and let it out slowly.

"Please, Asa?"

He closed his eyes and turned the ignition. "Fine. But I'm letting Anthony know so he can tell Mr. Lambourne."

"No problem. I'm not trying to worry anyone. All I want is to go to the beach. It won't take long."

Asa made the call and then we started on our way to Santa Cruz. It might have been a long drive for the five minutes I planned on staying, but it was what I needed for William and me to start fresh. I sat back, fingering the plain gold band Jace had given me on our wedding day. I'd kept it safe in the bottom of my jewelry box the past few years, and not knowing how long we would be at Casa di Rosabela, I'd packed the jewelry box and brought it with me. The ring felt warm and hard against my hand and in the bright spring sun, it glowed a burnished gold. We'd been through a lot together, the ring and me. This would be our last trip.

*****

Asa must have really been heavy on the pedal because we made it to Santa Cruz in about an hour and a half. I'd been so lost in my thoughts that I'd missed the mountain scenery and the famous redwoods as he'd navigated the winding expressway through the mountains and then down toward the coast. I could see the ocean now, sparkling in the distance, and knew if I opened my window, I'd smell the familiar scent of the sea. It was all so familiar and it should have calmed me, but it didn't.

I stared out my window, watching the signs for Spanish-named streets pass as we inched our way in traffic. The palm trees and groupings of whitewashed stuccos buildings with red tiles roofs reflected the Spanish mission influence here, and everything about Santa Cruz looked the way it always had. But I was seeing it through different eyes now and it no longer felt like home.

I'd grown up in Santa Cruz, gone to college here, and my parents both still lived here. All of my firsts had happened here, too. I rode my first surf board, bought my first camera, and I'd learn how to combine my love for both here. I'd fallen in love, then had gotten married here... and then I'd spent over two years here lost and buried in my grief as a widow after Jace had died.

And then I'd left. It had been almost exactly one year ago that I had moved to Chicago.

We passed the river, and the famed boardwalk with its roller coaster, and then the wharf as I directed Asa toward the neighborhood where I used to live and to the beach where Jace and I had always surfed: Pleasure Point.

I had Asa find a parking spot near the little park that sat on a bluff above Pleasure Point.

"I just need a minute, okay?"

"I'll wait right here."

"Thanks." I climbed out, still in my heels and my bridesmaid dress, which whipped around me in the wind. That earned me a few curious looks from people hanging out in the park. I kicked off my shoes, grabbed them, then gripped a handful of my dress and hiked it up. I didn't want to trip as I descended the wooden stairs to the beach below, which wasn't much of a beach at all. It was more like a rocky outcrop that jutted out into Monterrey Bay. The surfers didn't mind the lack of sand, since the nice break just offshore was what drew them here.

There was a rock shelf to sit on and it had always been my favorite place to perch and watch Jace while he tried out a new board or worked on a new trick. He'd spend hours in the water and I'd spend hours watching him or taking pictures of him. Even when he'd wipe out time after time after time, he'd keep getting up, back on his board, ready to catch the next set. He'd loved being out there and that kind of drive and dedication is what helped to make him a champion. I'd always admired that about him. Always.

I couldn't sit today—my thin silk chiffon dress was no match for the slippery, wet rocks—so I stood and held my shoes and the hem of my dress and looked out over the water. Most of the surfers were done for the day, but a few still caught some waves. I knew if any of them came closer, I'd probably see a few old friends or surfers who'd known or aspired to be Jace. But that wasn't why I was here.

Carefully, I stepped to the edge of the rock and dipped my toes into the freezing ocean. Tears stung my eyes, but I didn't bother to hold them back.

We'd had so many good times here, Jace and me. And yeah, a few arguments, too. We'd laughed, cried, fought, made up, made love under the stars, woken up with the sunrise, and paddled out into the bay side by side. It had been a good life. I'd loved Jace so fucking much.

And I'd always love him. But we'd had our time and it was…over. As much as it hurt, I had to let Jace become the beautiful memory that he was. My first real boyfriend, my first husband, and the first person I'd loved so hard with my entire being that it had hurt.

The first, but not the last. Now it was time for me and William. I loved William in that same hard, all-consuming way and I knew that he loved me back just as much. It was time for me to accept all of it and let that love flourish. I pressed a hand to my belly, thinking of the life already flourishing there.

"Goodbye, Jace," I whispered to the waves breaking unceasingly against the shore. "I love you."

I clutched the gold wedding band one last time, lifted it to my lips and kissed it, then flung the ring hard. It flashed in the lowering sun and disappeared into the blue water with a tiny splash. I knew Jace would understand. The man I'd known would want me to be happy and I would always remember him for that.

I stared at the faraway spot for a long moment, then I wiped the tears from my cheeks and straightened my shoulders. I felt like the last burdens I'd carried were finally gone.

I was free.

I climbed back into the car, and smiled at Asa. I'm sure I looked an absolute fright with my bare feet, windblown hair, and tear-streaked face, but I didn't care.

"Everything okay, Miss Cat?" he asked with concern.

"Yes. Everything is perfect now. Asa, can you take me home? To William?"

"My pleasure."

NINETEEN

Saturday evening
William

I'd come down to the olive grove for a few minutes of peace. Most of the guests had gone and the few that lagged behind weren't leaving until tomorrow anyway. I wasn't needed, and though clouds were rolling in and humidity hung in the air, it was still a perfect evening to stroll among the rows of trees. This was one of my favorite spots on the entire property and I always found sanctuary here.

I knew Catherine was fine. Asa had called and said she'd asked him to take her to Santa Cruz. She'd lived in Santa Cruz. With Jace. I didn't know exactly why she felt the need to go there today, but I had a vague idea. Whatever she was doing in Santa Cruz, I hoped it would bring her some peace and that she would be ready to talk when she got back.

Meanwhile, the wedding was over and Beckett and Alec were on one of my jets and on the way to Tropos. I'd called in a favor with Sir Nigel, and the island was the newlyweds' for the next ten days. I hoped they enjoyed themselves as much as Catherine and I had.

I'd taken her to that very private luxury retreat over Valentine's Day, and it had been one of the best times of our lives.

I'd known I loved her long before that, but those few days in paradise had given me a taste of just how good things could be between us. I'd never wanted it to end.

According to Catherine's doctor, it was pretty likely Catherine had conceived on that trip, so we'd brought a souvenir home with us.

A baby.

Our baby.

It had surprised the hell out of me, but I wanted it all—the woman I loved and the family I never thought I could have. Fuck if I was greedy. I didn't give a shit. I would have already taken what I wanted if it was that easy. But it wasn't. Catherine had shown me just how complicated and scary life could be. And the irony was, I already knew. Losing my parents and Wyatt had taught me that years ago.

I turned to look back at the house and saw my beautiful girl walking toward the olive grove. I'd wanted her and she was there. She took my breath away. The sun was almost down, and the last pink rays of light tinged her with a rosy glow. The breeze caught the fluttery silk of her dress, making it cling to her body. As she came closer, I could see the slight curve of her belly. I hadn't noticed it before, but it was right there. Our child.

I grasped a tree trunk and leaned against it for support. A lump had risen in my throat, and my legs felt unstable. She was so beautiful, and I had the privilege of watching her blossom right in front of me.

The olive trees swayed in the wind, making a soft shushing sound, interrupted only by the soft patter of Catherine's shoes. I could smell rain in the air, and it was sweet and tangy.

"Hey," she said, coming to stand before me.

"Catherine."

"I'm sorry I left like that. I came to tell you I forgive you for telling Zoe about the baby." She spoke quickly as though she wanted it all out. "And I wanted to apologize, not just for leaving with Beckett, but for last night."

Her face looked pained, and I took her hand, not wanting anything to ever cause her pain. "Catherine—"

"Let me finish." She squeezed my hand. "I know you love your family, William. I know what the Smiths mean to you and why they're so important. I've been selfish and not trying hard enough with Zoe. I'll do better, I promise. I know how important she is to you."

I nodded, hoping that was the end because all I could think about at that moment was kissing her.

"And I know you love me, William. I know you want to keep me safe, but the past few weeks and you not touching me have felt like a rejection." Her voice hitched, and I swallowed to keep from pulling her into my arms. "I need you more than ever, and I want to feel close to you. I need that closeness. You won't hurt me or the baby. And that's another thing."

I tried to stifle my sigh. At this rate, I'd never kiss her.

"We need to talk about the baby. You and me. We said we'd

wait to tell people, but I didn't think that meant we'd stop talking about him. He's real, William. I want to talk about him. And I want to tell everyone!"

I pressed my lips together, but she could probably see the corners of my mouth twitch. "*He*?"

"Just a feeling I have. Here. Feel this." She pressed my hand against her belly. The curve I'd seen when the wind caught her dress was tangible under my palm. "I'm starting to pop out a little. Feel it?"

"Mm-hmm." I looked down at my hand, covering her from hip to hip.

"I'm okay. He's okay. We're okay, William. We're not going to lose him. The universe wouldn't do that to us. We've both lost enough, I think…" Her voice trailed off. Maybe she'd finally talked it all out. The wind rattled the leaves again, and the first raindrops plopped against my arm.

"It's going to rain. We should go inside," I said. Even as I spoke, more drops plinked on the ground.

"Not yet. There's something else."

Of course there was. But Morrison had said women needed to talk. So we'd stand in the rain and talk, if that was what she needed.

She looked up at me, and her tears mixed with the raindrops splashing on her face. "I lost something precious to me once, and I'm not going to let it slip away from me a second time. That was where I went today. I needed to say goodbye to Jace one last time. And I did. So now, I'm ready…" Her voice trailed off as she looked up at me with her impossibly beautiful green eyes.

"William Maddox Lambourne, will you marry me?"

My heart lurched in my chest. I'd probably just had a minor heart attack.

"I can't imagine my life without you and I want to marry you. I want to very much. You're my everything, William. Just name the time and place, and I'll be there."

The words were too much for me to take in at first and my throat constricted and my eyes filled in response. I'd wanted them so much I almost couldn't believe them. The rain fell in sheets now, washing away both of our tears but soaking us, too. Still, it felt like nothing could touch us. My fear seemed to dissolve with each drop.

Finally, I allowed myself the grin I'd been holding back. "Absolutely, beautiful girl. And thank you."

acI didn't risk that she had more to say. I crushed her against me and kissed her as much to silence her as because I needed to feel her lips against mine. I wanted her, but I wasn't going to stand in the rain any longer. I swept her into my arms and started back for the house.

Catherine laughed and kissed me again, and the salt of her tears mingled with the fresh rain on our faces.

"I will marry you, beautiful girl, but there are a few things we need to do first."

TWENTY

I carried her into the house and straight to the master suite.

I kicked the door closed and lowered Catherine to the floor. She reached for me, but I caught her hands. "You're cold and wet. Let me fix that."

She lowered her hands to her sides, and I stripped her out of the wet dress, her bra, and panties. Then I lifted her again and carried her to the bed. I pulled the covers back and nestled her in its warmth before shrugging off my own wet clothing. Catherine's eyes were on me the whole time, feasting on my body in that way I loved.

Finally I lowered myself to her, but instead of taking her mouth, I slid down and kissed her feet. She laughed and wiggled because her toes had always been a little ticklish.

"I plan to kiss you from head to toe, beautiful girl. Every. Single. Inch. Of you." I worked up from her toes to her slim ankles and her muscled calves. When I kissed the back of her knee, she moaned. I'd learned early the back of her knees was a sensitive spot for her. And then my lips were on her silky thighs, the skin so soft I thought it would melt when I touched her. I didn't ignore her pussy, but I kissed it only briefly.

I'd come back.

I lingered on her hips and her rounded belly, kissing her tenderly there before I moved to her breasts. God, her tits were magnificent. They'd always been amazing, but the pregnancy had made them larger and rounder. Her always sensitive nipples were swollen like small pink cherries, and I wanted my tongue on them. I wanted those hard buds in my mouth.

I feasted on one breast, fondling the other, sucking until her hips moved against my hard cock. She wanted me inside her, and I wanted to be there, but not yet.

"William, *please*."

I almost gave in because the need in her voice practically undid me. Instead I kissed her, my tongue stroking hers as my hands wandered her body, moving up and down over her curves and slopes.

Finally I slid back down again. I wanted to worship her body, every single thing I loved about it and the way it was changing, too. She was so lush, her skin so soft. Finally, I parted her legs and slid my fingers over her sweet pink center. This was my favorite part of her and she was wet and glistening for me.

I dipped my tongue down to taste her sweet nectar, loving the slide of her slick skin on my tongue. I parted her lips and gently pushed back her hood to reveal her swollen clit. I swirled my tongue over her once or twice before she bucked, hands fisting in the sheets. I put my hand on her opening, feeling more wetness pool there.

I started a slow, teasing lapping against her clit, coming at it from above and then underneath and then sucking it into my mouth.

My fingers slid inside her tight, hot channel, and I worked her gently, sucking and nipping. I loved the feel of her sex against my mouth and the way her body trembled and her legs wrapped tightly around my shoulders. She rocked against me, pressing hard to my lips, her hands in my hair, urging me forward. This time when she came I dipped my tongue inside her to feel the tremors and taste the sweetness of her orgasm.

I could have done this all night, but I wanted to be inside her. I knew she needed that now, needed the connection between us. And I needed it, too. I levered myself on my elbows and looked down at her.

Her eyes were hazy and unfocused, her face flushed. I pushed her legs apart and settled my cock at her entrance. Her eyes opened when I breached her opening. She couldn't ignore that.

Her arms pulled me close. "Yes," she moaned, rocking her hips up.

I entered her slowly, my eyes locked with hers. I let her feel every single inch of my cock entering her, filling her. It was like I was finally returning home after a long journey. She closed tightly around me, sheathing me until I had to groan and grit my teeth to maintain control. Her hands touched my face, stroked my cheeks, and all the while I moved inside her, I never looked away from her eyes.

In and out I slid—into that wet, velvet fist and out again, relishing every moment of connection between us. I nudged her legs apart further and lifted my body to hit her where I knew she liked it.

She clenched around me, and I could barely hold back. But she came first, I thought, over my body's screaming pleas to fucking come already.

"I love you," I said, just before she crested and her face turned impossibly beautiful with the ecstasy of the orgasm I gave her.

"I love you, too," she murmured, and that was all I needed. I let go, spilling into her with a growl. Everything went dark for a moment, and then I rolled to the side and gathered her into my arms.

"I missed you," she said.

"I'm back," I murmured, cupping one of her breasts. I was not going to be able to keep my hands off them. I circled her nipple, and she sighed.

"Do that and you'll turn me on again."

"I can't help it. Your tits are amazing."

"They're bigger and fuller. I guess so I can feed the baby when he's born."

"I'll be jealous."

She glanced up at me and I shook my head. "Just kidding. I can share you…for the most part. Besides little Wyatt needs to eat."

"Wyatt?" She propped her head on her hand. "Is that what you want to name him?"

"I thought it might be nice."

"I do, too." She settled back and snuggled into me. "Wyatt William Lambourne."

"No. Too many Ws."

She frowned at my tone. "Wyatt Beckett Lambourne then."

I gave her ass a light slap. "I like Beckett but not *that* much."

"We'll keep talking."

I looked down at her and kissed her lips. "Yes, we will." I had it all now—Catherine, a baby, the vineyard. Anything else would just be icing on the cake.

ABOUT THE AUTHOR

Sorcha Grace is an adventurous eater, beach lover and author of scorching contemporary erotic romance. She is also the nom de plume of a nationally bestselling author who publishes in another romance genre. Find her on Facebook and Twitter.

www.facebook.com/SorchaGrace
Twitter: @SorchaGrace

www.ingramcontent.com/pod-product-compliance
Lightning Source LLC
Chambersburg PA
CBHW011229120626
46549CB00008B/3203